THE

BOOK THREE IN
THE CALLING SERIES

CHOOSING

L.C. PYE

The Choosing

Copyright © 2024 by L.C. Pye

Contact Info: authorl.c.pye@gmail.com

Front Cover Design by: Selkkie Designs

Editor: E&A Editing Services

ISBN: 979-8-9879746-4-3

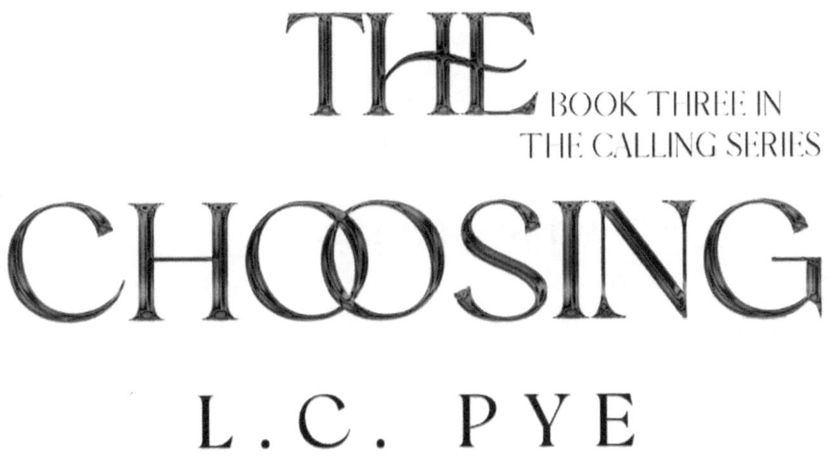

THE CHOOSING

BOOK THREE IN THE CALLING SERIES

L.C. PYE

LiftedLines Press

SIGN UP FOR MY

AUTHOR NEWSLETTER

Be the first to learn about L.C. Pye's new releases and receive exclusive content.

*Dedicated to those needing to make a difficult choice.
Follow the peace in your heart.*

KINGDOM
NORTH
KINGDOM OF TRO'ISH
KARDEN
BANESMYTH
HATTLEE
THE CLEARING
GASMERE

LANDORE
AYDENCIA
OUNTAINS
LLYCIA
KINGDOM OF
NEFALI
CYPERIAN
SEA
KINGDOM OF
VASDERE

Chapter 1

Talia

THE FLOORBOARDS CREAKED BENEATH my feet, their protest blending with the hum of the sea. I widened my stance to steady myself against the sway of the ship. The familiar motion no longer startled me; instead, it soothed me. With each ebb and flow, the distance between King Madden and me grew, and my hopes of being free from his control gained strength.

A deep moan pulled my attention to the only bed in the captain's cabin where Raph lay against the wall. The morning sun, nearly over the horizon, peaked through the small circular window and shone over him. I set down the supplies Eitan had secured from the nearest village, for Raph's wound, and made my way over to the bed.

"Raph. Wake up," I whispered. "Raph..."

I held my breath and his eyes opened briefly, then closed again. My heart raced as my hand hovered above his bare shoulder, suddenly feeling awkward about touching his skin. I shook my head. He was a patient. I gently touched his uncovered shoulder, letting myself feel the warmth from his skin. I gave him small shake.

At last, his emerald eyes opened. He was dazed, but gradually he focused on me. I parted my lips to say something, but the earnest look in his eyes stopped me. I withdrew my hand, suddenly very aware that we were alone.

"I need to stitch your wound," I said, shifting my gaze to where his injury was located.

"It's fine," he said. His voice was raspier than normal. "I'm sure it's not that bad." He attempted to push himself up and groaned.

"What do you think you're doing?" I placed my hand back on his shoulder to press him down, knowing he would try again.

"Seeing what the damage is," he hissed between gritted teeth while he resisted my hand.

Perceiving how stubborn he was going to be, I gave up and let him prop himself against the back of the wooden bed. The blanket slipped, revealing his strong, bare chest. Heat traveled up my neck. There was no denying he was attractive, anyone with eyes could see that. However, it was the voice in the back of my head telling me there was more to it than attraction that had my insides twisting. My blush deepened as I realized I was still staring at his bare chest. I averted my eyes to the bandage I had wrapped around his waist. My stomach dropped when I saw the blood had seeped through. The wound he had received the night before from fighting off the King's Guard to escape was deep.

"Stop." I smacked his hand away from the bandage. "I'll do it."

He snorted and opened his mouth like he was going to make a comment, but he frowned and brought his hand to the dark bluish-purple bruise along his ribs.

"I think you might have broken a few." I turned toward the wooden desk in the middle of the room and grabbed the makeshift tray I had assembled with the supplies to stitch his wound.

"Nothing I haven't dealt with before." He went to raise his shoulders but dropped them with a hiss as I made my way back.

"So, this happens a lot with what you guys do?" I asked, making sure my eyes stayed off his chest as I placed the tray on the edge of the bed. I let the silence continue to see if maybe he would let something slip about who they really were.

He combed his fingers through his chestnut-colored hair, leaving it annoyingly disheveled. "Let's just say this isn't my first time being stitched up."

I fixed my eyes on the blood-soaked bandages, focusing my mind on the task at hand. His head fell back, and a sharp inhale filled the air between us as I peeled away the bloodied fabric.

"I'll be quick," I said as his body remained tense. I set to work cleaning the wound, thankful to be doing something to distract my mind from whatever was wrong with my stomach. I had thought about him, and the others, often while imprisoned by King Madden. There were so many questions I had and things I wanted to say. And here he was right in front of me, yet I couldn't help but feel nervous and awkward.

The cloth shook in my hand as I felt him studying me. Out of the corner of my eye I noticed his gaze moved to the oversized green tunic Adira gave me. His eyes widened before he redirected them back to my face.

The moisture in my throat evaporated. "I...I'm going to start the stitches." I grabbed a piece of leather from the tray and brought it close to his mouth.

"I don't need it," he said and moved his gaze to the ceiling. He gave no audible signs of pain as I sewed his skin back together, but the tight grip he had on the blanket told me he wasn't immune to what was happening.

I tied the last stitch. "There," I said, scanning over my work. A small sense of pride bloomed in my chest, knowing Mother would be proud.

"Not bad." He peered at his side. "It's a lot cleaner than the last stitch job I got."

I arched my brow, but he didn't give in to my curiosity. However, I had noticed the numerous scars his upper body bore. There was a prominent one on his forearm that pulled my attention, it resembled a burn. I narrowed my eyes, curious as to how he must have received such an injury.

He cleared his throat, breaking the silence between us. I flushed and fought the urge to hide within myself as I caught a glimpse of the amused expression on his face.

"I—" I licked my lips. "I learned from the best Healer in Gasmere," I replied, then busied myself with placing the materials back on the tray. The contents clinked softly as I placed everything back on the desk. I rubbed the back of my neck and peered through the small circular window behind the desk, wishing for it to open and allow the winter air to bring me relief.

"What is she like? Your mother."

A sharp twinge shot through my chest as I tried to find the right words without ending up in tears. King Madden's threat of no one being out of his reach still rang through my ears. I had no idea what he planned to do next since my escape, and I had no idea where my parents were, or if they were even safe. It felt like an eternity since my maids, who were secretly aligned with the Northern Rebels, had promised to have some-one get my parents to safety. And with a botched escape attempt at the ball and weeks of pretending to be both a princess and Prince Kasper's fiancée, before finally breaking free myself, all I wanted was to know they were safe from King Madden.

I sat at the end of the bed, clasping my hands in my lap and pushing those thoughts aside before they unraveled me. "My mother is the most caring, selfless, and stern woman I have ever met." I shook my head, pushing a loose piece of hair behind my ear. "Both of my parents are wonderful," I added, unable to stop my lips from turning up. "They saved me," I shrugged. "I was an unwanted baby left in the forest to die. But they took me in." My smile faltered as I lowered my gaze. I didn't know why I felt the need to share all of that with him. "I owe them everything." The fear for their lives tightened its hold around my heart.

"You'll see them again," Raph said, placing his hand on top of mine.

His touch was so unexpected that I almost pulled away, but I let his hand warm my cool skin as I yearned for his words to be true. Despite his gentleness, I could sense the underlying strength within him, like when he held me in his arms in the forest. I had felt safe then, as if everything would be alright. Something I desperately needed to feel again.

"What about your parents?" I asked, pulling my gaze to the floorboards.

He withdrew his hand from mine. I had to catch myself from reaching out to grab it again. "There isn't much to say. I never knew my father, and my mother loved me the best way she knew how," he said, turning his face upward, toward the plain wooden slates. "She was always sick, and when I was seven, she passed away."

I bit my lip. "What did—"

The door slammed against the wall, causing us both to jump. Raph released a groan, and I stood.

"He lives!" Gil swung his arms out wide in a silly flare. I had to stifle a nervous laugh. "Trying to steal my job as the dramatic one?" he asked, perching on the desk while taking a large bite of a piece of fruit that Eitan had picked up in the village.

"Wouldn't dream of it," Raph replied between his teeth as he pushed himself higher on the bed.

"At least have the decency to put a shirt on." Gil winked at me. I rolled my eyes ignoring the tightness in my stomach.

"Mind finding me one that isn't already being worn?"

I followed Raph's gaze to my tunic. I pressed my lips into a firm line, promising to have a serious talk with Adira. The green in Raph's eyes darkened as I tugged at the hem of the tunic, suddenly wishing for one of the ridiculous gowns I wore in the palace.

"Glad to see you're back to normal," Adira said as she entered and threw a shirt at Raph's face. Jules and Eitan followed close behind.

I moved to stand near Jules, still needing the reassurance she was actually there and this wasn't all a dream.

"When will we reach Aydencia?" Raph asked while he pulled the shirt over his head, his movements stiff and awkward. The room remained quiet. Pausing his task, Raph zeroed in on Gil first before ending on Adira. "Well?" he asked, pulling the tunic down.

"I ordered them to head to the nearest village to pick up supplies," I said, but my voice seemed to be swallowed up by their stares, and my last word was a near whisper. I looked to Jules for help, and she gave me an encouraging nod. "And we," I gestured to Jules, "have decided that before you take us to your hideout, we will be stopping in Gasmere."

"Is that so, Princess?" Raph's brow rose as he swung his feet to the floor.

"Yes." I narrowed my eyes. "The village is in danger." I stepped closer to him. "King Madden threatened to burn it to the ground if I disobeyed him. We must warn them."

Raph stood. "You think Madden isn't scouring the entire kingdom for you? That he hasn't sent his guards and his pet wraith out to find you?" His voice matched my own in desperation. "They aren't going to let the lost princess and the prince's fiancée just disappear." He balled his hands into fists. "I'm not letting you go anywhere near where he could find you again."

My fight dampened slightly at his confession, wondering why he truly cared for my safety. Wondering what I meant to him. My thoughts briefly went to the letter he had sent to me in the palace before I squared my shoulders, dismissing the thought that he meant what he wrote. "And I'm not going with you unless we go to Gasmere first," I said, reigniting my resolve.

The others stayed quiet as we stared at one another. Raph showed no sign of backing down. His stubbornness bothered me to no end.

"We're only about a day from Gasmere," Gil said with a full mouth, breaking our standoff.

Raph shook his head. "We need to ensure her safety. We head for Aydencia."

Jules stepped forward. "We can't let a whole village be burned to the ground."

"And we can't risk Madden getting his hands on the lost princess again. We are going to Aydencia," Raph repeated.

"I'm right here." I waved my hands, gaining Raph's attention again. "And how are you going to make me go?

Are you going to threaten me like the king did to get what you want?"

Raph's facade faltered as if my words had wounded him. "Tali—Princess, we are trying to protect you."

"Then you'll take me to Gasmere first. I need to know they are safe." My voice caught in my throat.

"I thought you said someone had already extracted your parents." Eitan said. He stood the closest to Jules and me with his arms crossed over his chest and a genuine concerned look on his face. I had given them a brief rundown of my experience with the Northern Rebels in the palace as we journeyed to reach the closest village for supplies.

"I never heard if they were successful. That was almost a month ago." I met Eitan's, and then Raph's eyes. I needed them to understand.

"It sounds like, from what you told us, the rebels in the palace are working with some of our acquaintances," Adira said with a side-glance at Raph. She stood on the other side of the desk, leaning her weight against it while fiddling with one of her blades. "They would have brought your parents to Aydencia."

"They're probably there waiting for you," Gil chimed in with a wide grin.

I reached my hand to my neck, only to place it around my waist, not willing to trust the hope that stirred inside me. "I have to be sure." I turned to Raph because no matter how much I hated it, he was the one who would decide what happened next.

The muscles in Raph's neck became visible. "Okay. We head to Gasmere." My shoulders dropped. He quickly added, "But only Jules, Eitan, and Gil will go into the village. The three of us will wait at the closest safe house."

I opened my mouth, but Jules spoke first. "Safe house?"

"Yes, we have multiple around the kingdom." Gil answered, giving the desk a love tap. "We had this old girl stashed by the one nearest Llycia. Madden never even knew." He flipped his hair back with a devilish smile, then threw the last bite of fruit in his mouth.

Jules gave Gil a penetrating stare. "And what exactly are these safe houses for? You have still failed to mention what you *really* do."

"We don't have time for this," Raph said, clutching onto the bedpost for support. "After we confirm your parents aren't there and we warn the villagers, we will head to Aydencia." He looked at me, and a bead of sweat dripped down the side of his face. "Do we have a deal, Princess?"

I should have ordered him to lie back down, or at least offered him a shoulder to lean on. But I stayed in place, smashing my lips into a straight line. "Yes."

"I will set the new course." Gil bounded for the door. Eitan and Adira followed behind him. I dashed out ahead of Jules, leaving her to close the door behind us. I didn't slow until my feet hit the top deck.

"Jules, want to help us secure the sail?" Eitan yelled from further ahead. He gave me a smile with a bow of his head. I covered my frown. Ever since they rescued me, things felt different.

"You good?" Jules asked as her hand reached out to me.

"I'm fine," I replied with a shake of my head. "Go." I nodded toward Eitan.

Jules jogged over to where Eitan and Adira were already working on dropping the sail. A hole in my heart ached as I watched, feeling more distant from everyone than I wanted to admit.

CHAPTER 2

Talia

"WE'LL REACH THE SAFE house before sundown." Gil peered into the distance through a spyglass.

The tightness in my chest lessened as I looked out in the same direction, knowing Gasmere wasn't too far away. The cool, morning wind pushed against me, and I clutched the opening of my cloak as I made my way to the helm where Gil stood. Everyone else was busying themselves with different tasks.

"Want a look?" he asked, lowering the spyglass.

I accepted it and placed the cool, metal ring to my eye. "I see nothing but water."

He chuckled, and then gazed off into the distance. "The Cyperian Sea knows no bounds," he said with a hint of mystery. He focused on me and seemed to cast off whatever he had been thinking. "You'll see land soon."

Giving Gil a look of disbelief, I leaned against the railing and brought up the spyglass once more. But when I tried looking through it, a motion from the corner of my eye caught my attention causing me to lower the spyglass. Raph made his way to the bow, pausing to clap Eitan's back as he worked on the ropes. My grip tightened around the spyglass. He should've been resting. I continued to watch as he tightened the ropes to one sail. The moisture in my mouth evaporated with each strong pull he made, and I told myself it was only because I was worried about his injury.

"Find a better view?" Gil asked.

I shoved the spyglass into his chest and made my way toward the side of the knarve before he could notice the blush I felt travel to my cheeks.

"It's okay if you did," Gil called after me in between laughs.

I wrapped my cloak around myself and focused on the white foam on the waves. But my gaze kept drifting back in the direction of Llycia, unable to stop reliving my time in the palace, where any sense of control over my life had been ripped from my grasp. And even though I was relatively safe here, I peered over my shoulder at the others. I still felt no sense of control.

I leaned my elbows on the railing, searching the horizon for answers, knowing I wouldn't find any. What

I needed was some sense of normalcy. I needed my parents.

"Oy, land ahead!" Gil shouted, cupping his hands to his mouth.

Squinting my eyes, I tried to see anything besides the endless blue in front of me. Adira and Raph followed behind me as I made my way back to Gil.

"Keep us out for as long as you can." Raph held out his hand for Gil to give him the spyglass. "They know we're traveling by water," he said, peering through it. "We will wait until dusk before dropping anchor." Raph passed the spyglass to Adira.

"Aye aye, Captain," Gil said with a mock salute.

While Gil was grinning at Raph's usual unimpressed expression, Adira offered me the spyglass. I snatched it. A small sliver of land magnified to reveal a beach that raised ever so slightly. As I moved my focus further down, I noticed something dark. It looked like a black cloud, but there were no other clouds in the sky.

"What's that?" I asked, pointing toward it.

"That should be close to where Gasmere is located," Gil answered, throwing an arm around my shoulder.

"But what is that dark cloud? Is a storm coming?" I handed the spyglass to Gil.

He looked and said nothing, but his arm dropped from my shoulder.

"Well?" I asked.

"Raph, take a look." Gil's voice dropped as he passed over the spyglass.

"What is it?" I grabbed Gil's arm, ready to explode if he didn't tell me.

"Smoke," Adira muttered.

"Yes," Raph confirmed.

"It can't be." I shook my head. "That would mean..." My heart stopped. "No. No..." I grabbed Adira's hand. "Tell me it's not..."

"I...I'm sorry." Adira's eyes were full of sympathy.

I covered my mouth and fell to my knees. A cold sensation from the floorboards traveled up my arm, penetrating my body, but I was already numb. Muffled voices echoed around me as I realized I was too late.

Swallowing the shock, I allowed Adira to help me to my feet. Jules ran up the stairs with Eitan behind her.

"What's wrong?" Jules asked. Raph handed her the spyglass. "No!"

"We have to go," I said, looking to Jules first and then the others. "All of us. We have to help them."

"It's a trap. Madden is probably doing this to lure you in." Raph turned away, dismissing me.

"I'm not asking." His back tightened, then he turned to me.

"You don't know for sure if Madden will still be there," Jules said, but Raph didn't acknowledge her.

"I'll keep my head down. No one will know it's me." My eyes bounced from Raph to the cloud of smoke. "I have to do something! This is all because of me," I pleaded, feeling the knife in my heart sink deeper. Raph's silence made my frustration grow as desperation crawled up my throat. "I'm going."

"Why can't you understand your role in this?" Raph raked his hand through his hair and then closed it in a tight fist. "You need to stay safe."

"Tals," Jules placed her hand on my shoulder. "Raph might be right. You are a princess now, maybe you should stay back?"

I shook off her hand.

"That doesn't mean I don't have a say over my life anymore." I widened my stance, looking back at Raph. "I will swim there if I have to."

He remained unmoving for what seemed like an eternity. "You will not leave my side." Raph spoke each word as a threat. "We will stay on the outskirts of Gasmere, understood?"

"Yes."

"If there is one sign of Madden or the prince, you will leave immediately."

I nodded fervently.

"Steer us to Gasmere." Raph stormed down the rest of the stairs.

Adira's hand landed on my shoulder. "He'll be fine. If anything were to happen to you, he would hold himself responsible."

"And I feel the same about those I love." I pulled away from Adira and walked down the stairs to the front of the knarve.

We didn't touch land till dusk. Raph refused to let us go ashore any earlier. I spent the day watching the sky darken with more smoke.

It was excruciating.

We walked for an eternity in the dark, our visibility hindered by the dense smoke that surrounded us. We attempted to shield ourselves from breathing it in by covering our noses with our cloaks, but it didn't stop us from coughing or our eyes from watering as we walked deeper into the thick cloud of smoke.

Jules signaled with her hand, and we drew toward her. "Gasmere is a little southwest of here," she said in a hushed tone.

Raph, who had been walking closer than necessary to me, gave her a nod of understanding. He then moved his focus to me, probably to make sure I was close enough for his liking. I took a step away from him as I kept my eyes on Jules.

"We are about half a mile out," Jules finished with a cough.

"The goal is to get in and out." Raph scanned everyone's face. "Don't draw any attention to yourself." His focus ended on Gil.

"What?" Gil said, readjusting his cloak to cover his mouth again. "I—"

"I think it would be best then if we split up," Jules cut in. Gil opened his mouth, but Jules spoke over him. "Eitan and I can enter from the Hunter's quarter. The rest of you can come from the fields in the Farmer's quarter. We will rendezvous back at the clearing." She shifted her gaze from me to Raph, who gave a nod of agreement. "Tals, are you okay with leading them there?" Her question stung. I wasn't helpless. She waited for my answer, and I dipped my head slightly.

"Let's move out," Raph ordered.

As Jules and Eitan veered north, Adira and Gil flanked Raph and me on both sides.

"Make sure you bring us around the back, where we will be least visible," Raph muttered under his cloak. "And remember you and I are staying by the border." I didn't even bother looking at him. I pushed forward toward my home.

As we crept closer to the boundaries of Gasmere, my chest tightened, and I couldn't shake the urge to run. A part of me hoped it was an accidental fire or a forest fire like the one that had happened when I was a little girl. The entire village had had to help to stop it from spreading into the town or the fields. It took days before the smoke had disappeared.

But the forest was quiet—too quiet. The only sound came from our labored breaths and footsteps. I couldn't deny the foreboding in the air, warning me to not come any closer.

We broke through the cover of the trees and into the boundaries of the Farmer's quarter.

I gasped and dropped the cloak from my mouth.

It was gone.

Past the fields were the remains of what were once multiple Farmers' homes. All that was left were the skeletal frames of houses—if that. Piles of black ash covered the ground, but they were slowly being stolen away by the breeze.

Desperation overcame me. I sprinted through the burned fields and up the dirt street, ignoring the voices behind me. I couldn't stop, nor could the tears streaming down my face. My name continued to be called, but it sounded far away like ghosts calling after me, haunting me for what I let happen.

I ran into the burned remains of my childhood home.

Smoke rose from a few areas. It couldn't have been more than a day since this happened. The kitchen was the only place where things were still recognizable. The metal pots and onyx stove sat like bones that refused to burn. Everything else was unrecognizable or ash.

I picked up a brass bowl and clutched it to my chest as I fell to my knees. I coughed when a cloud of ash blew up. I gripped the bowl tighter, lowering my head.

I yearned to hear my parents' voices fill the space around me. To hear Mother scold Father for forgetting to pick something up at the Penta again, and then for him to shower her with compliments to earn her forgiveness. I wanted it to go back to the way things were. Before Jules got kidnapped.

I lifted my head to where our kitchen table once stood. My vision blurred as I remembered the last conversation I had with Mother before everything changed.

It was before my calling ceremony, Father was out in the fields. Mother and I sat at the table chopping vegetables for dinner. "Talia, whatever may come next for you, know that you're who you are meant to be. And your father and I will always be here for you." I could hear Mother's voice as if she was sitting right next to me in this pile of ash. All I could think about was how untrue her words were. Because of me, they weren't here when I needed them the most.

"Talia," a voice called.

An arm wrapped around my shoulder, and I flinched. Peeling my tear-soaked eyes from the remains of the table, I discovered Adira kneeling beside me. Over her shoulder was Raph and Gil. Both were unable to hide the horror on their faces as they observed the destruction around them. I leaned into her embrace, and she tensed, but she didn't move away as she took some of my weight. A sob broke out. For the debris around me showed how I already felt on the inside. Destroyed. There was nothing here for me to come back to. My old life was gone, and worst of all I had no idea if my parents made it out.

I let the sobs rack through me.

"Welcome home, Princess."

I dropped the bowl with a thud at the unexpected voice.

Chapter 3

Kasper

THE SOUND OF HORSES' hooves striking the ground resonated behind me, mirroring the intense beating of my heart. We traveled with no rest for two days, and I felt my horse's strength wane. But I urged him to the front through the dense smoke, determined to reach camp quickly after the scout mentioned it was a short distance ahead.

Breaking through the trees, I pulled tight on the reins.

"Whoa."

I dismounted and threw the reins at the nearest guard, not glancing in his direction. I allowed my black cloak to trail behind me, focused on finding out what had transpired in my absence as I made my way through the camp that was set up outside the village's borders.

Guards dropped whatever they had been doing to bow when I passed by, but I didn't slow my pace until I pushed the flap of the tent open.

"Report," I barked at the guard who was in charge until I arrived. Father dispatched his men nearest to Gasmere the moment Talia escaped with those rebels while I was unconscious.

"Every quarter has been destroyed, Your Highness." The guard's voice shook as he lowered himself into a bow. I pressed my tongue to the roof of my mouth, preventing any emotion from slipping out. The guard stepped away from the table he had been peering over.

"And the princess?" I asked, moving toward the same table in the middle of the tent, where a large map was. I didn't need to turn around to know he had taken a few steps away from me.

"She...she is nowhere to be found."

The sliver of hope that she might have already been discovered died as I placed my palms on the table, letting it take some of my weight. "The people who claim to be her parents?"

"They have not been located either, Your Highness."

I slammed my fist on the table. "Leave me," I roared as the table shook underneath me.

The guard retreated out of the tent. I rubbed my forehead, trying to rid myself of the pain that had been plaguing me since I woke from the sleeping tonic. It had been three days since she escaped, and if I didn't find her...I let the thought drop before it could spiral.

I scanned the map of Landore, wondering how I was back in the same position—searching for the lost princess, my fiancée. I shook my head at the thought of our almost wedding, still in disbelief that she had drugged me.

When I felt the effects of the sleeping tonic, I knew she was trying to escape again. The dread that had been suffocating me since my father announced our engagement lessened as I let the tonic do its work without alerting anyone, but then I woke in the Healer's wing with Sal standing next to my bed. He joyously informed me the king was waiting for me with a special little treat.

With a guttural roar, I flipped the table across the tent. How could I think I'd ever be free from my father's threats? I stormed out with one thought in mind.

To find Princess Talia and return her to my father.

The twenty-plus guards who accompanied me had arrived, most of them were resting on tent bags instead of setting them up. They needed rest, but it wouldn't come—not yet.

"Sal!" I yelled into the haze of smoke encompassing the whole forest.

A few of the guards stopped what they were doing and scurried away in different directions, most likely to find him. I went back into the tent, and it didn't take long before Sal limped in, still favoring his left foot thanks to our run-in with the rebels. He kept his hand possessively attached to the sword at his hip. It was a present from the king himself, beautifully crafted with the hilt's fancy design covered in gold. I clamped my teeth together. My father never gave gifts, at least not of that kind.

"Your Highness," he said with a small bow, but cynicism was thick on his tongue.

"It's time to make our presence known in Gasmere. And I need to know that you will adhere to the king's plan."

Sal's hand flexed and relaxed on the pommel of his sword. "I have yet to disappoint my king, Your Highness."

My glare transferred from the sword to his face. "We can't afford any accidents like last time," I said, dropping my gaze to his lame foot.

Sal's chest rose as his grip tightened around his sword. I remained unbothered by his show of frustration. We had never gotten along, but I didn't fear Sal harming me. He was smart enough to know the best way to beat me was having me take the blame for any failings and, in turn, he'd win my father's favor, something that had been happening more and more recently.

"Have the men gather the villagers in the Penta," I ordered.

His eyes narrowed. "Right away, Your Highness," he said, leaving the tent. Within minutes, the sound of them vacating the camp site echoed around me. It would be easy to rid myself of Sal permanently, but my father's guards were loyal to him. For he had been their captain before my father bestowed the *honor* to me. They only followed me out of fear.

I released my breath as I stared at the map in front of me, wondering whether Princess Talia was even still in Landore. The rebels could have taken her anywhere by now. But after studying her over the past month, I knew she wouldn't leave without making sure those she cared about were safe. *That* was her weakness. And I knew exactly what my father would command me to do—find those she cared about. I moved away from the map and headed into the village.

It was unrecognizable. Though I hadn't spent a lot of time in it previously, every village appeared the same. Five quarters branching out from the main localized area where the villagers did their business. I had entered from the Hunter's quarter and everywhere I looked was ash. A wooden beam crashed to the ground to my left, filling the air with debris. My father was a man of his word, and he had warned her that this would happen if she disobeyed him. The blame was hers.

"We don't need your help!" A man in green balled his fists by his side as a guard pulled a sobbing woman from the remains of her home. She clutched a small metal cup.

I watched as other Hunters came to stand behind the man in green. I changed my trajectory. This was exactly what I'd warned Sal about. My father's orders were to aid the villagers, to gain their trust and loyalty.

A different guard stepped toward the small group and withdrew his sword. "Disperse. Head to the Penta."

I sucked a breath between my teeth when none of the villagers moved and the guard took another step forward.

"What's the problem here?" I asked from behind the two guards.

They bowed their heads and the villagers' eyes doubled in size. A small sob broke out. A little girl had been hiding behind a villager. Her eyes focused on the woman held captive by the guard. When she became aware of my stare, she hid behind the villager's legs.

"We were assisting them to the Penta as you ordered, Your Highness," the guard replied, still holding the woman by the arm.

"At the moment, it looks like you're doing the exact opposite of *assisting*. Let her go at once," I ordered.

The guard released his grip.

Heat traveled up my neck as I looked at the villagers. How was I supposed to gain their loyalty?

"Mama!" The little girl ran into the woman's arms.

"My apologies, ma'am," I said, lowering my head to the woman. "The king offers his condolences to this whole village after the tragedy you have faced. We are here to assist in the matter," I said with what I hoped resembled a smile.

The woman said nothing as she lifted the little girl and turned away. The rest of the group followed, casting wary glances over their shoulders.

Once they were at a safe distance, I seized the collar of the guard who had restrained the woman and drew him in. "We mustn't use force of *any kind,*" I emphasized. "You are to show compassion. Is that clear to you?"

His eyes widened, but he said, "Yes, Your Highness."

I looked at the other guard, who gave me a quick dip of his head. "Clear out," I ordered, releasing the first from my grip. "Make sure every guard knows what's required of them." They gave a bow of their heads and left my side.

I watched them scurry down the path and pulled at my sleeves. The relentless pounding in my head grew stronger as my patience thinned. My fingers instinctively flexed as I took my first step toward the Penta. The anticipation of what I had to do next built with the sound of my feet hitting the dirt path. I needed answers from the villagers, and quickly. It was only a matter of time before blood would be spilled. I rolled my head to the side, cracking my neck. Becoming a love-sick fiancé was the last thing I was prepared to do.

CHAPTER 4

Talia

THE FIRE INSIDE ME exploded as Jacob Martin stood on the road with the same wolfish grin that haunted my dreams as a child. He wore that look whenever he was gearing up to make my life worse. But there was one big difference I couldn't ignore: he was dressed in a crimson uniform. He was a guard.

I rushed him before anyone could react. When I got close enough, I punched him in the face. Searing pain consumed my hand, but the overwhelming rage within me masked the agony.

Someone yanked me off my feet and carried me away from a livid Jacob. But I didn't let it stop the rage from pouring out of my mouth. "You weasel! You spineless good-for-nothing fool! What did you do?" The suffocating grip of the arms around me grew stronger, leaving me unable to wiggle out of their hold. "What? Reporting me wasn't enough? You had to burn your own village to wear that uniform?"

For one second, Jacob's eyebrow met in confusion, but then his eyes narrowed as he wiped blood from his nose. He stepped forward with a snarl.

"Don't take another step," Raph ordered, holding me tight to his chest.

"You either," Gil said, stepping forward with his bow drawn. That is when I noticed the two other King's Guards standing behind Jacob. They were young and somewhat familiar. They lifted their arms with fear plastered over their faces.

Jacob's nostrils flared. And then his whole demeanor shifted. "It was your house that went up in flames first when they came looking for *you*. *You* caused this, Caffrey, not me." His arms stretched out to the surrounding ruins. "My mom was right. She always said you'd bring nothing but trouble to this village."

I launched forward and almost out of Raph's eased grip, but he quickly latched back on to me.

"Now, now..." Jacob raised his hands in front of himself. "Wouldn't you care to know if they survived or not?"

"Where are they?" I meant to yell it, but my heart caught in my throat, and my words came out as a croak.

He rocked to the balls of his feet, then sauntered closer. I heard a bowstring tighten.

"Raph, let me go," I ordered under my breath.

His arms loosened. I could feel him press closer to whisper in my ear, "If he makes one wrong move, I'll carry you out of here myself." His words lingered before he finally released me completely.

Jacob closed the distance between us and leaned down as though he was passing a secret. "The last thing I heard were their cries over the roar of the flames as I watched your home burn to the ground."

"Liar!" I shoved him. "You're lying!"

His brown eyes filled with excitement as he peered over his shoulder where more guards were making their way toward us.

"Princess," Raph shouted. "We're leaving."

I let my fingernails cut into my palms. The one thing I knew was that Jacob Martin loved to lie, whether it was to get out of trouble or make someone's, often my, day a lot worse.

"Talia!" Raph grabbed my arm.

"Okay." I turned to follow when someone grabbed my other wrist.

"No you don't." Jacob pulled me toward him. He glanced over his shoulder at the guards who had taken notice of us and were closing in. "I know someone who is anxiously awaiting to be reunited with you." The sides of his lips lifted.

I twisted and pulled, trying to break his grip.

"Ahh!" Jacob yelped and dropped his hold on me.

I fell into Raph and stared as Jacob's hands went to his thigh where a small dagger protruded out of it.

Raph yanked me behind him and yelled, "Run!" Adira and Gil flanked us as the group of guards gave chase.

Raph kept his firm grasp on me, even as we hit the smokey tree line. I wasn't worrying about which direction we were headed in. My mind was consumed with my interaction with Jacob, dissecting each word he said to see if there was any truth in them. We ran until a small whistle shrieked behind us. Raph pulled me into a bush, which caused me to land on top of him.

I tried to slide off, but he gripped my hips tighter.

His hot breath hit my cheek. "Don't move," he whispered.

Adira and Gil were nowhere in sight and as we lay hidden in the bush, voices grew closer. Raph tensed beneath me, and his grip on my hips tightened.

I closed my eyes and held my breath, trying to ignore the adrenaline coursing through my veins, heightening my awareness of the intimate position we were in. I refused to acknowledge the weird way my heart pounded. However, being able to feel the rise and fall of his chest brought a sense of comfort I would never admit out loud.

Minutes passed, but they felt like an eternity as we silently waited till it was safe. The voices faded into the distance, leaving an eerie silence. Raph's grip slowly loosened, but he didn't remove his hands. A soft whistle filled the air. It could have easily been mistaken as a bird, but Raph pushing me away was confirmation.

"What's going on?" I whispered as we stood.

"Gil gave the all-clear. We lost the guards."

"But where are they—"

Gil fell from the sky, landing feet first in front of me. "Don't worry, we were never that far," he said, giving me a wink. "By the way, great hit back there." He gave me a friendly punch in the arm with a broad smile.

Hitting Jacob had felt great, despite the pain radiating in my knuckles. It was something I dreamed about doing for years.

"They headed toward Gasmere," Adira said as she landed next to us. I scanned the high branches of the tree she had been hiding in.

"We need to move. They could be getting horses to continue their hunt," Raph said. He walked like he expected us to follow. "We need to get back to the knarve and make our way to Aydencia."

"What about Jules and Eitan?" I stopped. "We can't leave them. What if something happened to them?"

"It's too dangerous. We can't risk you getting caught." Raph didn't cease walking nor slow down.

"Raph, stop!" I said, marching up to him.

He spun around and came mere inches from my face. "No, Talia, you stop," he snapped in a harsh whisper. "For once, stop running into every situation blind, and trust me." His chest heaved. "I need you to realize you hold the freedom of thousands of lives in your hands. This is about so much more than you and your family."

I staggered back. "I didn't ask for any of that. I want to be safe. I want my family to be safe. I want Jules to be safe. And even you guys." A hot tear fell down my cheek. "I can't worry about anyone else right now, especially not a whole kingdom." I wrapped my arms around my waist. "I know it's too dangerous for me to go back into Gasmere. But I will not leave Jules and Eitan. Can't we hide and wait for them at the clearing?"

Raph's expression was unreadable. He rubbed a hand down his face. "We will stay hidden in the clearing while Gil and Adira search for them," he commanded.

I released the breath I had been holding as I nodded my head in agreement.

"Lead the way, Princess," Raph said, gesturing with his arm.

"Where are they?" I asked, wringing my hands as we hid behind a grouping of dense trees. The comfort I was hoping to feel was nowhere in sight. The clearing carried the memories of Jules and me spending our time there practicing and talking about anything and everything, but as I tried to visualize each memory, they become tainted, transforming into a sad reminder that it would never be the same.

"Shh," Raph said, scanning the area for guards from behind one of the trees. "It was *your* idea to stay and wait."

"Excuse me for being concerned." I crossed my arms over my chest. He continued to peer out in the distance. "I just found out that my home was burned to the ground, and I still don't know where my parents are. I'm not going to lose Jules as well."

"We already told you, your parents are likely in Aydencia, where we should be," he said the last part under his breath. "Jules is with Eitan, she is fine. And the villagers can always rebuild."

"It's winter. The ground is freezing. And you don't know for certain where my parents are. King Madden could have them for all you know." I couldn't hide the hopelessness in my voice.

"He doesn't."

"You can't know that!"

He looked over his shoulder at me. "If he did, he wouldn't be bothering with all of this," he said, waving his hand in the smoky air. "He would use them to draw you out."

His gaze moved back to scanning the area. I pressed my lips together, wanting to argue back but I couldn't, because he was right. And knowing that my parents weren't in King Madden's hands was the only thing keeping me from unraveling. I resumed wringing my hands but stopped as a thought crossed my mind. "Why doesn't any of this bother you? You seem like you couldn't care less that hundreds of people just lost their homes."

"I never had one," he said with a shrug of his shoulders, peering through the trees. "So, it doesn't mean the same to me."

"You've never had a home? But before your mom passed—"

"We bounced around in Llycia for two years, mostly staying in whatever accommodations we could find for the night."

"What about before Llycia?"

"I don't recall."

"After she passed?" I wrapped my cloak tighter around me.

He turned to fully face me. With an exhale he lifted his gaze up to the sky before bringing it back down to stare me right in the eye. "I became a street orphan."

"But I thought you lived in Aydencia—"

"Alon found me." The side of his lip turned up. "Well, I should say, Alon caught me trying to steal from him when I was thirteen. He offered me a job and a different way of life. I took it and never looked back." His voice hardened at the end.

"How long did you live on the streets?" I asked, taking a tentative step to him and hoping he wouldn't shut me out.

"Six years."

"Raph, I can't imagine...to be that young and all alone..."

"I survived," he said, crossing his arms. His walls were up, but I felt the weight those two words carried. It had cost him greatly.

Not knowing why, I moved closer, and to my surprise, he didn't back away. He stood against the tree, staring at me. I was close enough to reach out and touch him, but I didn't. I stared back, not knowing what to say or do.

A snowflake gently settled on his long lashes.

He didn't move and neither did I. Soon, his dark hair transformed with a thin layer of glistening snow. Despite the frigid air, a wave of warmth spread through my entire body. My stomach churned with a mix of nerves and something else. He moved from the tree, closing the distance between us. His gaze never left mine as I slowly, almost unconsciously, tilted my chin upward. My heart pounded in my chest, a wild rhythm that contrasted with the silent snowfall.

Without warning, he moved past me and walked into the clearing. Heat flared in my cheeks at the realization of what almost happened—and that it didn't. That he had walked away.

The sound of footsteps caused me to look over to where Raph stood. Gil and Adira were running our way. I forced myself to stand next to him and put what happened behind me. It was probably in my head anyway, at least that's what I tried to tell myself, but that thought made me feel even worse.

"They're holding some sort of meeting," Gil announced breathlessly.

"Every villager was brought to the Penta," Adira finished. "We couldn't stay. There were King's Guards everywhere."

"And *he* was there." Gil looked at me.

The three of them stared at me. I didn't need Gil to say his name.

"We will give them an hour. If they don't show, we're leaving," Raph stated, leaving no room for an argument. But I wasn't going to give one. The fear of knowing he was so close had everything in me screaming to get as far away as I could.

Jules and Eitan needed to hurry.

CHAPTER 5

Jules

"No." I SHIVERED, WATCHING as he prowled across the platform like a predator eyeing their meal. My kidnapper. The King's Wraith. The crown prince. Somehow, all one and the same.

Eitan nudged me, but it wasn't until the third time that I realized he was trying to get my attention. I peered into his deep brown eyes staring back at me with obvious concern. I shook my head and refocused on the man covered head to toe in black, which contrasted against the white layer of snow that coated the platform.

We stood near the edge of the crowd, in case we needed a quick getaway, but that meant I could only see half of his face. It was more than enough. I flicked my focus over the crowd. No one had uttered a word. Yet from their expressions I could tell, I wasn't the only one seeing their nightmares come to life.

He lifted his hands and pushed back his hood, and somehow the silence became almost tangible.

"People of Gasmere." His voice was low, yet it filled the air. "What transpired last night was a great tragedy. The moment word reached your king, he dispatched his men here to give aid." He cleared his throat. "However, the danger is still out there. King Madden does not want you to be unaware of the actions behind a certain rebel group any longer."

Eitan scoffed next to me.

"Earlier in the year, you may have heard reports of young women going missing around the kingdom, and I'm here to confirm they were true. The same rebels who burned your homes to the ground last night were the ones who also kidnapped young women."

A few gasps echoed through the crowd. A mother near us grabbed her two daughters, bringing them close. I shook my head. How could anyone believe these lies?

"You might ask yourself, Why? And why Gasmere?" he asked, continuing to address everyone. "It has been in search of the lost princess," he paused, "my fiancée, Princess Talia." No one gave much reaction, which confirmed my suspicions that after the ball, all of Landore had become aware of the lost princess.

The King's Wraith tugged at his collar. "That is why I stand before you as a broken man, searching for his fiancée." I crossed my arms with an eye roll. His recited words carried no genuine emotion. "For on the night of our wedding, a group of these same rebels kidnapped Princess Talia. We believe they came here looking for her parents and burned the village to the ground to send a message."

"Come on," I said.

"Shh," Eitan whispered as those around us looked our way.

I bit down on the inside of my cheek and shoved my fists into my pockets.

"If anyone has information about this dangerous rebel group or Princess Talia's parents, we ask that you come forward." He extended his arms toward the sides of the platform, where there were two sets of stairs.

No one moved.

He dropped his arms and rolled his neck to the side with an exhale. "These people are dangerous and will do the same thing they did here to other villages. They need to be stopped." His voice raised. Finally, an actual emotion broke through, anger. "I know one of you has information." He paused. "Fine. I will give you some perspective." He reached for something on his hip. But then he froze before withdrawing it fully. I followed his line of sight but couldn't see what he was staring at.

Finally, movement on the other side of the stage stole my attention. Someone was moving toward the platform. A guard limped up the stairs, which broke the vacant stare the King's Wraith had. He glared at the guard, but the guard didn't seem to notice or care as he faced the crowd.

"As you can tell, the crown prince is a desperate man searching for his bride."

I threw a hand to my mouth to stop myself from crying out. The guard was Sal. A flash of that night came without warning. I heard her blood-curdling screams. I tensed and my breathing became erratic. Eitan placed his hand on my shoulder and the weight of it helped ground me a little.

"But like His Highness mentioned, we are looking for any information that someone might have on this group of rebels or the whereabouts of Princess Talia's parents." Sal's words and smile were more believable than the prince's, but his tight grip on the hilt of his sword didn't go unnoticed. "For your protection, King Madden orders you to be wary of strangers and to report anything to the guards that will be stationed in Gasmere until this is over." That got a reaction from the crowd. People turned to look at each other, but he continued, "Your safety is of the utmost importance to the king. And to show that, he has opened spots for a place within his guard for any well-abled man or woman to help protect Landore and its people."

"What about helping us rebuild?" a voice called out from the crowd, followed by a chorus of mumbles in agreement.

Sal and the King's Wraith both whipped their heads toward the voice before sharing a look. Sal cleared his throat, and the scattered voices lowered. "Landore's safety from these rebels is our priority. After we catch them, I'm sure the king will provide everything needed to help rebuild this village," Sal said with a tense smile.

"But it's winter!" another voice called out.

"All our storehouses were burned to the ground. We won't have enough food!"

Everyone broke into shouts. I stumbled forward as someone pushed me from behind. Eitan grabbed me before I could fall. The crowd pushed toward the platform, yelling out their fears and concerns.

A loud crack echoed across the Penta. Silence followed.

The King's Wraith stood tall with a whip in his hand. My heart rate spiked. His expression alone kept everyone silent.

"The penalty for anyone found conspiring against the king by harboring information about the rebels is death. Anyone with information will be rewarded. Greatly."

Whatever stillness held the crowd evaporated as a wave of whispers grew. Ignoring it, I kept my focus on the platform, watching the King's Wraith. It was like the time I came across a wolf during a hunt. I watched its every slinking movement, keeping an eye for any sign it had noticed me and would pounce.

A guard ran up the platform and whispered something into the King's Wraith's ear. I studied his face, catching his eyes widening ever so slightly before they narrowed again.

"You're dismissed," he commanded, descending the platform. He shouted something to the guards nearby, but I couldn't hear it.

I glanced back to the front of the stage where a smaller crowd was forming. My father and mother were right in the middle of it. Father was talking to the anxious villagers. I wanted to run to them to let them know I was alright. But I needed to find Tals first.

"Let's go." I nudged Eitan to make our way back into the forest.

"Maybe they went back to the knarve," I said to Eitan, eyeing the clearing. My chest tightened at the sight of it. I was wrenched back to the moment of being kidnapped. I came early to get some practice in before

Tals joined. It had been a warm day, and I lifted my hair from the nape of my neck as I bent to retrieve one of my arrows. But everything after that was blank until I awoke in that wagon.

Shaking those memories from my mind, I refocused on the clearing. It had stopped snowing and with it the smoke had dissipated a little, giving us a better view, but even with the fresh coat of snow covering the clearing's floor, I couldn't see any signs of the others. "We will give them—"

Something, or someone, made a noise in the tree line across from us. We drew our weapons. I held my breath, needing it to be Tals and the others. My mind raced. What if they found her? And that's why he rushed off the platform. I felt my heart hammer against my chest as I kept the string pulled tight, focusing my gaze toward the tree line, ready to release my arrow at a moment's notice. Eitan and I shared a quick glance. He held his sword with a firm grip.

The noise drew closer, cracking twigs and rustling leaves echoing through the stillness of the forest. Time stretched as we waited for the unknown entity to reveal itself.

"We aren't looking for a fight. Well, not with you two." Gil stepped out from behind a tree with his hands raised and a sly grin on his face.

I released the arrow.

"Woah." Gil ducked as the arrow skimmed past the top of his head. "What was that for?"

"Sorry, it slipped," I said, placing the bow over my shoulder as I fought to suppress a smile.

"Good shot," Eitan said with a low laugh.

The others came into view and followed Gil toward our direction. Relief coursed through me at the sight of Tals, but it didn't last.

"He's here," I said to her.

"We know." She peered over her shoulder as she tightened her arms around her waist.

"They are blaming everything on you guys. Saying the rebels were the ones who were kidnapping the young women. They're saying they kidnapped you," I nodded to Tals, "and burned Gasmere down in search of your parents."

"No one will believe that," Tals said and gave a sideways look to Raph. "Right?"

"It doesn't matter. We need to move out," Raph declared. "By now, the prince will know you are in the area."

"That might have been what that guard told him before he dismissed everyone," I said, looking at Eitan. "But how did they find out?"

"Jacob Martin." Tals clenched her fists.

I mirrored her look of annoyance. Jacob was a bully to everyone, thinking he and his family were better than everyone else, but he had always had a specific hatred for Tals.

"We can talk more on the knarve," Raph said, turning around. Everyone followed.

"I'm not going." The words left my mouth before I even fully realized my decision, but I knew it was what I needed to do.

Tals was the first to turn around. "What?" She rushed toward me. The others hung back. "What do you mean?" she demanded.

"You saw it. It's our home." Talia's eyes dropped to the ground. "I need to stay back and help." I reached for her hand, as though I could convince her through touch that my mind could not be changed. "I can help rebuild what we can or help move women and children to other villages."

"But..." Her eyes darted, like she was trying to find an excuse for me to come with.

"You don't need me. You have them." I dipped my head to the four standing behind her. "And you have to go. You need to stay safe and far away from the prince and the King's Guards."

"But you won't be safe. He knows you too. He probably knows how important you are to me." Her fingers tightened around mine, but I felt how her hands were shaking.

I couldn't give in. I didn't want to leave her, but I needed to stay behind and help the village, hoping that would fix the constant tightness in my chest. I thought it would go away after we saved Tals, but it hadn't. "Don't worry about me. I'm not his concern, *you* are."

"I can't leave you. He will use you to get to me!" Fear glistened in her eyes. I reached with my free hand and grabbed her other one.

"I'll be okay," I said with a faint smile, ignoring my quickening heart rate.

"I'll stay with her," Gil announced, startling us as we turned to find him standing over our shoulders. "I'll stay behind. One of us should anyway. We need to keep tabs on what the prince is up to." His gaze flicked to Raph, who gave a small nod.

I wanted to object, but the moment he offered a sense of relief washed over me.

"Promise me you'll stay as far away from him as you can," Tals begged while squeezing my hands till they hurt. "Don't give him the chance to use you against me."

We stood there, knowing that I had broken the last promise I made to her. If I had stayed and watched over her parents, we might know where they were. Her mouth pursed in that way it did when she was trying to hold it together, but her eyes gave her away.

"I promise," I said under my breath with as much intensity as I could muster and with every intention of keeping this one.

"We have to go," Raph ordered.

Tals pulled me into her arms.

"You've got this," I whispered. "You can handle anything that comes your way."

She squeezed tightly before releasing her arms from around me, her eyes misty as she pulled away.

"Come here," Gil teased, pulling Tals toward him. She fell into him with a grunt. "I know it will be hard not having me with you, but don't worry, I'm sure you'll be able to find entertainment somewhere." He squeezed her tighter.

"I'll miss you too, Gil," she said, her voice a little breathless.

"Enough." Adira pushed her brother out of the way as she gave me a quick hug. "Stay safe. And please keep him out of trouble," she whispered in my ear before pulling away.

"I'll do my best," I said, giving a hopeless side-eye to Gil.

Eitan followed Adira with his own hug and encouraging words. Raph, however, stayed back, his eyes fixed on Tals. Sensing my stare, he gave me a quick nod.

"Let's move out," Raph said. Then he turned around and added, "And Gil, try not to cause too much chaos."

"I'll miss you too," Gil answered. He smothered Adira in one final hug and came to stand next to me as we watched them disappear into the tree line.

CHAPTER 6

Talia

I was taken aback by our sudden arrival at the shoreline. Lost in my thoughts about leaving my home and Jules, time had slipped away unnoticed. The forceful wind, free from the shelter of the trees, whipped through my braided hair, causing the loose pieces to obscure some of my vision. Raph and Eitan heaved a small rowboat toward the rough water where the knarve awaited us amid a cluster of boulders.

"Wait!" I called out.

Adira was the first to turn. The other two didn't stop their work, but they looked in my direction.

"I...I don't think I can do this."

"What?" Eitan called back into the wind.

"I..." I let my words die out. They placed the boat on the rocky shoreline.

"What's wrong?" Adira asked, coming closer.

I clutched onto my cloak, using it as a shield. "I can't go with you."

"We don't have time for this." Raph shook his head. "We need to get onto the knarve before that storm comes." He pointed to the west where a mass of dark clouds headed our way.

"Raph, the storm is moving fast. It's not worth the risk," Adira said, giving a side-glance in my direction. "Let's head to the safe house and wait it out."

Drops of rain fell from the sky.

Raph took one more look toward the approaching storm before pressing his lips into a line. "Let's move."

We stashed the rowboat in the trees, then headed north. I followed behind Eitan and Adira with Raph on my heels. We moved through the trees at a light jog, able to receive some cover from the rain. The storm easily caught up with us. We were completely drenched when Adira and Eitan came to a stop in front of a small rundown shack. I searched the area, expecting there to be something else.

Eitan didn't hesitate to open the wooden door, which was attached by one hinge. We quickly walked through while he clutched it, fighting against the wind. Raph and Eitan closed the door together and then secured it with a piece of rope that was lying on the floor.

The wind whistled through the holes scattered about the walls. "This is the safe house?" I asked.

There was nothing inside, no table, stove, or bed. Just a littering of dried leaves and evidence that animals had been around. It was an empty, abandoned shack. I wrapped my arms around my waist, fighting the chill from not only my wet clothes but the uncertainty that the roof wouldn't collapse on top of me.

"It wouldn't be that safe if it drew attention, would it?" Raph said and the floor creaked loudly as he walked to an empty corner of the room.

Shifting my weight, I tried to find sturdiness beneath my feet. I was afraid that at any moment the floor would give way.

"This place isn't safe. It could fall on our heads any second," I answered back, giving the leaky roof a once-over.

"Relax, Princess. You'll be safe." Raph lifted a section of floor and revealed a hole in the ground.

I flicked my gaze upward with a sharp laugh.

"This is the cover," Adira said, coming closer to me. "The real safe house is underground."

I looked back at the hole and swallowed the lump in my throat.

"It's not too bad." She shrugged her shoulders.

"Yes, says the girl who enjoys being in the dark," I said under my breath, eyeing the hole.

"Come on," Adira said with a small upward pull of her lip, nudging my shoulder.

Eitan took the secret door from Raph, who, without hesitation, lowered himself into the hole.

"You're next, Princess," he called up. I narrowed my eyes in his direction but all that could be seen were his fingertips reaching out of the hole. He really needed to stop calling me princess.

Not having another choice, I tiptoed toward the hole. Peering into it, I saw the silhouette of Raph's face staring back at me. My stomach tightened. I couldn't see anything else, not even the ground he was standing on. "If this is a joke and there isn't anything down there, I'm not forgiving any of you."

Adira and Eitan chuckled behind me, but I was serious.

"Just hurry," Raph said from below.

With a loud exhale, I carefully lowered myself, searching for the ground beneath me. Raph gently encircled my waist, guiding me as I descended.

A sliver of light filtered through the opening above and cast a dim glow on Raph's intense gaze. His hands lingered on my waist. Warmth exploded in my chest as he moved them slowly to my hips before he turned his attention upward. In one swift motion, he pulled me aside right as Adira leaped down. Her landing was quickly followed by Eitan's arrival and the sound of the secret door above us closing. Then darkness enveloped the space.

"Someone tell me this is not where we are going to wait out the storm," I said, looking over my shoulder as a small gust of wind touched my cheek, but the utter darkness prevented me from seeing where it came from.

"Adira." I jumped, startled by Raph's closeness as he called out her name.

"I'm working on it," she replied in a strained voice.

There was a shuffling sound back toward the opening and then a few sparks lit the space. Another second passed and then light emitted from a torch in Adira's hand.

"Got it," she said, moving to the opposite side of the hole, which seemed to be a tunnel of some sort.

I flinched when a hand gently touched my shoulder. Eitan looked down at me and gave me a nod in the direction Adira was headed.

I followed her through the narrow tunnel. With every step, a sense of unease settled in and amplified the already overwhelming feeling of confinement within the pungent earthy scent that surrounded us. But before fear of where they were taking me could fully take hold, the tunnel widened to reveal a circular chamber. Adira approached a table and ignited the lantern resting upon it, then securely placed the torch she held in a wall-mounted holder.

The room was about the same size as the shack above us, however there were two cots, some wooden crates that surrounded a small table, and a few more crates stacked against the dirt wall.

"Welcome to our safe house," Eitan gestured to the space.

Still scanning the area, I took a seat on a crate. "Ar...are they all like this?" I stuttered out between my trembling lips. I hadn't realized how wet and cold I was.

"Yeah, basically," Adira answered as she rummaged through one of the stacked crates. She pulled out bundles of clothing and threw some at Eitan and Raph who were still standing near the entrance. Raph grabbed the torch on the wall and then walked back through the tunnel with Eitan at his heels.

"We need to get out of these wet clothes," she said, placing a tunic and pants on the table in front of me.

Even with the dry clothes on, my whole body shook. Adira sat next to me, pushing her wet hair out of her face. My hair was halfway out of the braid it had been in, but I didn't have the energy to fix it.

"How are you feeling with everything?" she asked, giving me a skeptical look as she resecured her weapons to her chest.

"Honestly, I feel like it's time you guys gave me actual answers. Especially if you expect me to leave on a ship with you and go to some secret rebel camp."

"Fair." She bobbed her head twice.

I leaned forward and stared at her with wide eyes.

"Okay." She laughed, putting her hands up. "First, Aydencia isn't a rebel camp."

"What is it then?"

"It's like a village but larger and more developed than you'd think."

"How is that possible? How hasn't King Madden located it yet?"

She smirked. "It's well hidden."

"I thought you were going to answer my questions," I said, giving her a pointed look.

"I am." She leaned forward. "But I can't really explain it. You'll understand when we take you there."

I dropped my gaze to my clasped hands. "And what do you want from me when we get there?" I asked, voicing one of my fears.

"We want to protect you." Raph's voice echoed across the small space. He and Eitan entered wearing a new set of dry clothes. "And the safest place, where Madden can't get to you, is Aydencia," he said while taking the crate across from me. Eitan grabbed one near the wall and brought it over.

I wanted to believe that they could protect me, but the thought of being safe from King Madden felt impossible. Plus, their protection didn't mean anything to me if I couldn't find my parents. And deep in my gut I knew there had to be more to all of this. There was something they weren't telling me.

I pressed my lips together. "How many are in the Northern Rebels?"

"Enough," Raph answered.

"She deserves to know," Adira said.

"She'll know when we get there," he replied.

"I already told Adira." I crossed my arms. "I'm not getting on that ship tomorrow until my questions are answered."

"It won't hurt anything if we tell her now, not compared to her finding out in a few days," Eitan said.

"Fine," Raph said. He matched my crossed arms. "Tell her our secrets."

Adira rolled her eyes. "And you accuse Gil of being the dramatic one." She changed her focus to me. "We don't call ourselves the Northern Rebels. That was something Madden came up with. I'm not sure what our numbers are." She looked to Eitan who shrugged. "I would guess around two times the population of Gasmere."

My mouth dropped. That would mean there were over two thousand of them. I closed my mouth, trying to imagine what their camp looked like.

Raph grunted, which pulled my attention.

"And what about you?" I said with a look in his direction. "How do you all fit into this? I mean, you're only a year or two older than me."

"You're right," Eitan said. "We aren't a group of random young people allowed to go on these insane missions." He paused and looked at Raph, but Raph continued to stare at the lit lantern in front of him. "Alon handpicked us to join him. We are warriors, the best to come out of Aydencia Academy."

"Warriors? An academy? So, there are more like you?"

"Yes," Eitan replied.

"And Alon? He is like, what...the leader?" I asked.

"More like a general," Adira said, squinting her eyes. "He oversaw our training before—"

"I think that's enough." Raph stood. "We should get some rest. I'll take first watch. We head out the moment the storm passes." He walked out without another word.

My mouth hung open. I had countless more questions to ask.

"He's right. We should try to rest. We can answer more of your questions on our way there," Eitan said, walking over to the crates. He lowered himself to the ground and used them to lean against. "You two take the cots."

Adira gestured with her head to the cot closest to the table for me to take as she moved toward the other one.

When I rolled over to face the dirt wall, I couldn't shake the uncertainty about their end goal. I believed they wanted to keep me safe from King Madden, but that wasn't the sole reason they wanted me in Aydencia. My time with the king had left me skeptical, and Raph's unrelenting determination to get me there had me questioning their intentions. It was clear they wanted something from me, or rather, from the lost princess. But what would they do if they found out I wasn't her? King Madden's declaration about me not truly being the lost princess flitted across my mind.

The thought of escaping and returning to Gasmere to join Jules in the rebuilding pulled at me. But what if my parents were really in Aydencia as they claimed? What if they were being held against their will? Finding my parents was my priority. I would pretend to be the lost princess for as long as I had to if that meant finding them.

Despite my exhausted body, the weight of the situation weighed heavily on me. My mind reeled over everything that was going on and prevented me from falling asleep.

A noise startled me from my thoughts. In the dim light from the lantern, I turned to see Raph waking Eitan. I rolled back around, but a shuffling sound close by compelled me to look back again. Raph faced away from me as he lay in front of my cot, most likely to prevent any escape attempts.

Sighing, I rolled back over. But I couldn't ignore his closeness. Soon my thoughts turned to the clearing and what almost happened between us. Was the only reason he stepped away because of Adira and Gil? If he hadn't, what would have happened? Was it something I wanted? Tightly closing my eyes, I shoved those thoughts from my mind and focused on Raph's steady breathing behind me. It wasn't long before I could relax enough to drift off to sleep.

CHAPTER 7

Kasper

"We're close to the borders of the next village, Your Highness," the scout said. I raised my fist in the air, and at my signal everyone stopped their advancement.

We had been traveling to different villages for four long days and had nothing to show for it. Instilling fear in them about the rebels hadn't got me any closer to finding Princess Talia or her parents. We needed a different approach, especially since we wasted a whole day searching for her and those rebels around Gasmere.

"Is something wrong, Your Highness?" Sal brought his horse next to mine. He straightened in his saddle, peering out toward the tree line that concealed the next village. "The king once told me that stalling is akin to mercy."

I glared at him. He thought himself so clever, but I had always seen through him. He was a vulture, waiting for me to fail so he could seize back his position as captain of the King's Guard. I would gladly give it up, but that wasn't part of the king's plan for me. No, his plan was to prepare me for the inevitable day when I would follow in his footsteps and become king. Even though, he never failed to remind me of how ill-suited and undeserving I was for that position.

Bringing my horse around, I faced the unit of my father's men. They were mostly older with years of experience, which told me exactly how much faith my dear father had in me. I tightened my grip on the reins.

"I'll be taking two of you with me into this next village tonight. The rest of you set up camp around the borders and wait for my next orders." I clenched my teeth when a few of them glanced at Sal before nodding their heads in acceptance. "You are to remain unnoticed or there will be consequences." Sal's lips pressed into a firm line, probably ready to speak out, but I didn't give him the chance. "Julian and Oliver, let's move out."

I directed my horse onward and then heard the quickening sound of horse hooves hitting the ground behind me. I may have picked the youngest and most inexperienced guards of all, but they were the two I trusted to follow my orders. And I needed to try a different approach to gain information.

"Your Highness." Julian said with a bow of his head, riding on my left as we moved farther away from the rest of the unit.

"First, you are to call me Kasper, not Your Highness. We are to blend in as villagers from Gasmere looking for a fresh start." This was the other reason I chose these two. Most of the King's Guards' parents sent them to the palace at a young age for a large sum of money, but these two hadn't been away from home as long. They would still remember how villagers acted.

"If I may ask, how is this going to help us gain information on the whereabouts of the princess?" Oliver asked from the other side of me.

"I'm not searching for the princess. I know where she will be." I could feel their gaze on me intensify. "We are looking for her parents. They are what will draw her out. And the villagers will be more open to sharing what they have heard to some poor homeless villagers from Gasmere as opposed to two guards and the crown prince."

"Excuse me, Your Highne—" I gave Oliver a pointed look. "Kasper." He swallowed hard like it was difficult for him to say it. "But if you know where the princess is, why don't we go straight there and get her?"

"Because so far we have failed to infiltrate the Northern Rebels' camp."

"She's in the Northern Mountains?" Julian's voice raised an octave. Everyone on the King's Guard knew what a fortress the Northern Mountains were. For an entire year, my father sent unit after unit to find a way to break through. Many came back battered and broken, if they came back at all. Although, I wondered if the ones he sent by sea simply chose not to return, aware of what my father did with their failures.

"Yes," I answered.

"I understand, Your...Kasper. I'm honored to be chosen." Oliver placed his hand over his chest and gave a small bow of his head.

"As am I." Julian copied the same gesture.

I stared forward but gave them a dip of my head to show my recognition of their sign of loyalty. "Now, let's find different clothing."

"Relax," I hissed under my breath. "Try to blend in." I picked up my mug of ale and took a drink as I eyed the different occupants in the busy tavern. Loud shouts pulled my attention to a table near the door where two men were standing nose to nose. The other man at the table jumped up and wiggled his way between them while trying to talk them down.

Oliver and Julian sat across from me with their eyes wide and backs pressed firmly against their chairs as they observed the different villagers around them. Julian fidgeted with the slightly small brown tunic we had gained along the way. Thankfully, we didn't have to wait long before we found a group of Farmers out along the village border.

No one in the tavern seemed to pay us, three strangers, any attention, which was probably best. I couldn't engage in conversation with any villagers with these two looking like they were about to bolt at any second. I scanned the room one more time and something strange caught my eye.

Two men were sitting at the bar engaged in a conversation, but they were from different callings. One of them wore the colors of a Healer while the other was an Artist. I tilted my head. During my travels for my father, I would occasionally see different callings associate with one another, but it was over business and nothing else. The Healer slapped the back of the Artist and they laughed loudly. Even the barkeep gave a few chuckles.

"I'm going to get us another round," I said, then stood. Making my way to the bar, I took the open seat to the left of the Artist. Neither of them noticed me right away, too consumed with their conversation. From the bits

I caught, it sounded like they were talking about their families. I waved the barkeep over.

"What can I get you?" he asked while wiping a mug. He was a burly man, someone fit to scare off potential fights.

"Three ales." The barkeep nodded and turned away. "And I was wondering if you had any rooms for three travelers?" I asked.

"Sorry, we're at full capacity. With what happened to that village down south..." His grip around the cloth he was holding tightened. "We've had an influx of people coming through."

"I understand." It also explained why no one seemed surprised by the presence of three strangers. "Is there any other place taking people in?" I asked, knowing that the Artist and Healer had turned their attention to us.

The barkeep gave a side-look to the pair.

"Excuse me, I couldn't help but overhear your situation." The Healer leaned over the Artist. "Where are you traveling from?" he asked.

I turned to face them. "My friends and I," I gestured over my shoulder, "are traveling from the south. Gasmere." I lowered my voice as though I was too sad to say it any louder.

They gave a glance to one another before turning back to me.

"How are things there?" the Artist asked. "We've heard rumors that everything was destroyed."

The barkeep placed three ales in front of me. I placed the payment down and took a drink. "The rumors aren't far off. We will have to rebuild the entire village."

The Artist pushed back his curls as they fell into his eyes. "I still can't believe something like that could happen to an entire village."

"You can't," the Healer scoffed. "I have a feeling things are going to get worse for all of us. They still haven't found her, thankfully." He barely whispered the last word, but I heard it.

Both men scowled, and I had to loosen my grip on the mug, remembering my role.

"I'm sorry we haven't even introduced ourselves." The Artist stuck out his hand. "I'm Anthony Grady and this old man here is David Colan."

"Yeah, only in years. Physically, you carry on like you're twice my senior," the Healer joked as he shook my hand.

"Nice to meet you both. I'm Kasper."

"Well, Kasper, you seem like a nice enough young man, and your friends, well..." We turned to look at Julian and Oliver who still looked as if they had seen a ghost. "They look as if they have been through a lot," the Healer finished. "If you want, you can come stay with my family and me for a time."

"Are you sure? There are three of us."

"Don't worry. The Colans have beds galore." The Artist placed his arm around the Healer. "You and Esther might want to think about turning some of that space into quarters for those coming from Gasmere."

"You're probably right." The Healer snorted, then turned back to me. "My family and I run the Healing House," he explained. "So yes, we have enough space for the three of you."

"That is very generous of you. We plan to stay a few days at most. I promise we won't be any trouble," I said.

He gave me a smile. "You are welcome to stay as long as you need."

"Are you sure you don't want to clear that with Esther?" The Artist gave him a warning look.

The Healer's face paled. "Why don't you and your friends finish that round and then head on over to the Healing House. It's the only one in the Healer's quarter. You can't miss it." He stood and finished his drink.

"Good luck," the Artist said while saluting his mug.

I couldn't help my interest in their relationship show on my face as we watched the Healer leave.

"You aren't the only one confused," the Artist said, putting his drink back down. "Hattlee is a little different from other villages."

"What do you mean?"

"A few months ago, right before the Harvest Festival, we had a terrible illness hit the entire village. It wiped out most of our people and many died." His face dropped. "David and his family did everything they could, but they are the sole Healers in Hattlee, and they could only do so much."

"Why didn't the Elders reach out to the king?" I asked, surprised. When I came through here last time, it was during the Harvest Festival, and everyone was healthy.

"They did, but no help came. They also reached out to the nearby villages, but they became worried about catching what we had."

I leaned forward slightly. "So, what happened?" I asked.

"Thankfully, a group of travelers came through." His face lit up. "They helped the Colans and were able to find the cause of the illness. One of them, well, she even saved my boy's life." He sighed, and his shoulders dropped like a weight lifted off of them. "Since then, it felt wrong to go back to the way things were. We went through something traumatic together. To then go back to acting like none of it had happened and only care about those within your own calling didn't feel right."

I stared, unable to form any words. If my father knew this, he would burn this whole village to the ground before any other village caught on to what was happening. The callings were the one thing that had stopped the rebellions after my father had become king. He always told me the callings were what kept things in order.

"Are you alright?" His eyebrows pulled down.

"Yes. That is quite the story. It's a good thing those travelers were passing through."

"Indeed." A pause filled the air between us as his thumb rubbed against the handle of his mug. He was probably rethinking whether he should have shared that with me. "Well, it was a pleasure meeting you," he said, then pushed up from his chair. "I'm sure I'll be seeing you around." He left with a dip of his head.

Biting my tongue, I grabbed the three ales. I was certain of who those travelers were, especially since it was after I left this village that we encountered the rebel group in the forest. Picking this town to infiltrate could not have been a better choice. I placed the ales on the table in front of Julian and Oliver.

"Drink up. I found us a place to stay."

CHAPTER 8

Talia

THE BRIGHT SUN MASKED the misery of the past five days of travel. We were fortunate to have avoided additional storms, but traveling by water was torture in itself. It was particularly frustrating when a certain individual viewed me solely as precious cargo incapable of assisting in any way, which fueled me even more to find different ways to distract myself.

"We're here!" Eitan stood next to me, pointing into the distance. I peered out in the same direction and tightened my grip on the helm as a gust of wind tried to pull the wheel to the left. Eitan had been instructing me on sailing, and it proved to be more difficult than I had initially imagined. Nonetheless, it was the one thing Raph didn't object to me doing, and it made the painfully slow hours pass by faster.

I attempted to glimpse beyond the enormous cluster of mountains ahead of us. As we drew nearer, a sense of insignificance washed over me. I had only ever caught faint glimpses of them from the palace and through the drawings Father sketched in the dirt while teaching me to read. These mountains were truly immense, stretching toward the heavens and spanning across the kingdom. How did one live amongst them with no open land to farm or forests to hunt in?

"What's up there?" I asked, pointing to the top of one mountain.

"Snow," Eitan answered nonchalantly before noticing the shocked expression on my face. "Don't worry, Aydencia isn't nearly high enough to be bothered by it."

"But you said Aydencia was located on a mountain, right?" I asked, referring to the conversations Eitan and I had over the journey.

"Yes, but like I said, it will make more sense when you see it in person." He took back the helm.

I trusted him, but I couldn't help but feel anxious. There was no sign of a port or a village anywhere. I removed my cloak, unsure if the warmth was coming from my nerves or the temperature. The sun wasn't even at its peak, but the air around me felt warmer.

Eitan turned the wheel and headed west when we were about a field-length away from the mountain itself. Adira and Raph made their way up to us, searching for something along the face of the mountain.

"There." Raph pointed to a part of the mountain that looked exactly like the rest. It was only when I squinted and tilted my head that I could make out a faded design of what resembled a tree.

"It's Aydencia's symbol." Adira came to stand next to me. "It represents wisdom, strength, and endurance. Three things every Aydencian lives by."

I nodded in response. The idea of an entire village upholding those three things was intriguing and it filled me with more questions, but my eyes stayed fixed ahead of us.

"Eitan..." my voice shook because he seemed to be steering us straight toward the very solid mountainside. A hand pressed against my lower back.

"Look." Raph pointed in front of me and kept his other hand on my back. "Right there, between the two rock formations."

I searched where he was pointing. "I don't see..."

But there it was. The mountain behind it hid the opening. To the unknowing eye, it appeared like one mountain, but it was two—one behind the other. We sailed straight through the opening and banked north, following the narrow pathway. Eitan steered us through its maze-like pass.

"It is why the king has not been able to discover us. Only a select few know the pathway into Aydencia," Raph said. I prayed he couldn't notice the blush on my cheeks as I realized his hand was still sprawled across my back. "You will be safe here, Princess." I stepped away, and his hand dropped. Every time he used that title I felt the divide between us widen.

I gripped the railing in front of me and peered up, allowing the massive mountains that loomed over us on each side to distract my thoughts. The channel we were sailing through was narrow and if I stretched my hand out far enough, I could probably touch the mountain. A shiver traveled down my spine at the thought of it falling on top of us. Shifting my gaze to the front of the knarve, I focused on the sharp bends Eitan sailed through effortlessly.

"Welcome to Aydencia!" Eitan cheered with his arms outstretched.

My jaw dropped when I saw not a small village, but a full-blown city—a haven.

The narrow passage we sailed through opened, revealing a vast valley encircled by towering mountains. The sight was overwhelming, with so much to take in at once. It felt as though we were nestled within a bowl, surrounded by lush mountains that contrasted starkly with the ominous, rocky peaks we had just traversed. Land stretched out on both sides of us, and in the distance, fields could be seen where people tended to the soil while animals grazed within the confines of a wooden barricade. It reminded me somewhat of a Farmer's quarter, but more open. Directly ahead a port awaited us, teeming with a multitude of ships similar to ours.

"How is everything still so green?" I asked.

"Aydencia is pretty different from the rest of Landore. We don't really have four seasons," Adira answered.

Then I wasn't imagining it. The air was warmer.

Eitan chuckled beside me. "Gil says we have two seasons. Dry and wet."

I opened my mouth for an explanation, but nothing came out as I took in more of the city.

Smooth clay homes with orange roofs were nestled against the mountain, each positioned at various elevations. Bridges and staircases interconnected different sections of the mountain, creating a complex design with no sense of order. It was surreal, beyond the reaches of my imagination, yet unsettling. The idea of dwelling without a firm foundation caused my heart to constrict.

We headed straight to a large protruding platform made of wood that was elevated above the water. Multiple people were on it, attending to other knarves, but there were three people standing on the edge staring in our direction. In the middle was the largest of the three, and his stoic stance told me exactly who he was—Alon.

My heart filled with what felt like relief when I realized it was him. Soon enough, I could make out Hafsa and Nadav standing next to him. I never thought I would see them again, and it almost felt like coming home.

Adira and Raph set to work lowering the sail and throwing ropes out to those on the dock. We stopped moving and soon there was a wooden board placed across the side, connecting the landing to the knarve.

"Come on, it's time you learned all our secrets." Eitan smiled at me while gesturing to the makeshift bridge.

"Talia!" Hafsa was first to wrap me up in an embrace. "What a pleasant surprise to see you here in Aydencia!" I took in her features as she pulled back and smiled at me with her warm, dark eyes. I couldn't help but be taken aback by her beauty and the markings on her face. I returned the smile, somehow forgetting how different she and Nadav looked.

"A surprise indeed." Alon's deep voice cut through. It held an air of unease. When our eyes met, he gave me a small smile and bowed his head, but his eyes were hesitant. He was exactly how I remembered, except for his graying beard being slightly shorter.

"I'm sure we will hear about it soon," Hafsa remarked to Alon.

"Take her to Skyhall," Alon said as he glanced in the direction of the various people further down the wooden platform toward land. They had stopped whatever they were doing and stared in our direction.

Hafsa let me go, but only to put her arm through mine. "Come, it seems you all have had a very long journey." She peered over her shoulder at the others. "We'll let you freshen up and then we can discuss everything over a hot meal."

My mouth watered. I hadn't had a proper meal for over a week.

She started walking me off the landing without waiting for anyone else. Nadav gave a shake of his head with a growing smile as we passed by. He followed right behind us. Peering over my shoulder, I caught Alon talking to Raph. They were both staring at me.

"My parents." I stopped in my tracks to turn back toward Alon. "My parents," I said louder so he could hear me. "They were supposed to be brought here by a Northern Reb...one of your people." A large lump formed in my throat as I waited for Alon's answer.

"We haven't received your parents or news that they will be coming," he said with a frown. "But many of our people posted around Landore haven't been able to send their regular correspondents with recent events involving Madden. He's been doubling down on his efforts to find us."

My shoulders caved forward as the breath in my lungs vanished. I should have stayed. I knew I should have stayed in Gasmere and kept looking for them.

"But if they are with one of ours, then I'm sure they are safe, and we will hear from them soon." Alon tried to give me a reassuring nod, but I felt like I was cracking apart. The pieces I had been trying to hold together, hinging on the hope of being reunited with my parents, fell.

"Let's get you cleaned up and some good food in you." Hafsa placed her arm back through mine, but I barely noticed as she led me away.

CHAPTER 9

Raph

WATER DRIPPED INTO MY eyes as I emerged. It had been too long since my muscles could relax in a warm bath. Despite the fact that my body desperately needed it, my mind couldn't rest. I had completed the mission. Not only did we find out what Madden was up to, but we discovered and rescued the lost princess. There was nothing else required of me. Yet, I couldn't stop the feeling of failure from latching on.

Throwing on a fresh tunic and pants, I secured two of my favorite daggers to my chest and snatched an overcoat. Alon was expecting me. He wanted a thorough report before everyone came together.

When I reached the entrance hall, I paused and looked toward the women's wing. It had been obvious from Talia's reaction on the pier that she was struggling with the news of her parents. Her face became ashen and her eyes distant as they looked back to the entrance we sailed through. I had to lock my knees and fight against the desire to walk down the pier to be close to her. I'd hoped, for her sake, that her parents were safe in Aydencia this whole time.

I took one step toward the women's wing, but then turned my head and forced myself to go straight to Alon's study. Adira was with her. She would be fine.

"Come in," Alon responded at my knock.

I pushed the door open. A sense of relief washed over me, freeing some of the tension that had built up over the past weeks. The familiarity of Alon's study grounded me with its circular walls covered with books from the floor to the ceiling. The only gap was filled with a fireplace that fought against the constant chill in the air from being this deep in the mountain. During my first years in Aydencia, I frequented Alon's study almost daily for disciplinary reasons. I'd pass the time by memorizing every inch of the room. Over the years it had never changed. Even now, after being gone for over three moon cycles, I knew where every single item was located.

But there was one difference. Alon's desk was a mess. He hunched over a scattering of papers with his hands pushing through his short, graying hair. He looked unsettled, and that was not usual for Alon.

"Is this a bad time?" I asked.

"No. It's fine." He kept his head lowered as he waved me in, still engrossed in whatever was in front of him. I stood with my arms behind my back by one of the two chairs sitting on the opposite side of his mahogany desk. "I'm eager to hear this report, especially since you left Gil and brought home Talia instead." He propped his chin on his intertwined hands.

I told him everything. How his speculations were correct, and that Madden was up to something. I told him about the ball Madden threw to make an announcement, though Alon's lack of reaction told me this wasn't news to him. As I continued to relay the details about the Shades involvement and how Adira discovered Jules, Alon remained impassive. He expressed no sign of surprise when I conveyed how Madden declared Talia to be the lost princess. The bit of information that finally gained a small reaction was news about Gasmere being destroyed and the prince being on the hunt for Talia and her parents.

"So, I brought her back to Aydencia knowing that this was the safest place for her, if she *is* the lost princess..."

"Hmmm." Alon stood from his chair. His fingers grazed the top of the desk as he made his way to the side of it. "Yes, Aydencia is the safest place for her right *now*."

"What do you mean?" I asked. The crease between Alon's brow deepened. My stomach tightened.

"It's too soon to say," he said in his usual cryptic way while rubbing his chin. I ignored the pain from biting down on the inside of my cheek. He was purposely keeping me in the dark, but I wasn't going to give in that easily.

"What's really going on, Alon? Why didn't you join us in Llycia?" I asked, unable to hide the betrayal in my voice. His excuse about Nadav and Hafsa still didn't sit right with me. There was more to it.

He looked at me briefly before hovering over the papers again. "I already told you. I needed to handle some matters here with Nadav and Hafsa."

"And what were they exactly?"

"We had to make some preparations." He lifted a paper and discarded it a second later.

"For what?" I asked, forcing my hands to stay relaxed.

"Not what. Who." His eyes glanced up at me. He had let something slip. Not letting that hint go to waste, I sorted through the puzzle pieces of information in my head. All the way back to when we were given the assignment of rescuing the kidnapped young women.

"You knew all along." I leaned forward, tightening my grip on my forearm. "You knew Talia was the lost princess?"

"I had my suspicions..." Alon lowered his gaze back to the papers in his hand.

"When? When did you know?" I asked, practically shouting.

"The first day we saw her in that clearing." Alon released his breath and analyzed me. "She is a replica of the late Queen Aleese."

"How did you know that? Why didn't you say anything?" My mind was reeling, trying to find some sort of justification for Alon's secrecy and for letting her go.

He didn't answer me. Instead, he walked toward the fireplace, grabbing a thick leather book from the highest shelf and paged through it. He placed it before me.

On the open page, there was a small portrait painted. The king and queen were sitting on their thrones while their three children surrounded them. I leaned closer to take a better look. Even though the portrait was faded, I could still tell that Queen's Aleese's face was almost identical to Talia's. The only difference was that Talia's nose was sharper.

"Madden had this same portrait revealed when he announced the return of the lost princess," I remarked.

Alon's lips pressed together as he dipped his head. "Yes. Talia Caffrey is the granddaughter of the late king and queen. She is the rightful heir to the throne of Landore."

My chest sunk inwards. I had thought and maybe hoped that there could be a chance that it was all a lie. That Talia wasn't really the lost princess. That Madden had made it up and found a girl that looked like the royal family and passed her off as the lost princess, or maybe even doctored the painting to look like her.

"Did you ever meet the late queen?" I asked. Alon's past had always been a big mystery—to everyone. All we knew was that he had grown up in the palace.

"Yes," he sighed but then straightened again. "We have little time," he said as way of changing the topic. "Now that we have found her, everything is about to change." He released a long breath. "It's finally time."

I straightened. For the past seven years I had waited for Alon to speak those words, half doubting they would ever come, but now that they did, I couldn't ignore the tightness in my chest.

"I must inform Richard and Hanna of the news before dinner." That was my cue to leave.

Before I opened the door, Alon spoke. "I trust you will keep everything secret until it's time to be shared?"

"Of course," I promised.

He opened his mouth to say more but closed it with a shake of his head.

I left and wandered around the halls of Skyhall, not sure what to do with the information I'd been given, especially knowing that Alon kept me in the dark about Talia's real identity and who knows what else. In need of some fresh air, I left the building. I allowed my subconscious to lead the way, barely aware of my surroundings, as I ran through the past few months in my mind. From the shocking arrival of Hafsa and Nadav in Aydencia until now. It all had to be connected. But what would the Kingdom of Nefali want with Talia? Not Talia. The lost princess.

I didn't realize where I was until everything around me became too familiar—Aydencia Academy.

I gazed up at the tall, imposing building. It felt surreal to think that after seven long years of dedicating my life to the cause, it was about to come to fruition. The intricate details etched into the walls and the towering spires gave it more of a palace feeling, but it was nothing of the sort. I saw the shared moments with the other students, and the countless hours I'd spent in intense training, relentless in my pursuit of honing my skills with every weapon imaginable. The Academy, with its vast halls and echoing corridors, witnessed my evolution from a mere orphan to a warrior. It had molded me into the person I was today, instilling in me the values of courage, discipline, and loyalty. As I stood before it, I couldn't help but feel a surge of uncertainty. I walked to the back entrance. No one was around. The students and faculty would be getting ready for dinner, which gave me the silence I needed to get my thoughts together.

"Raph!" a man's voice called out.

I shifted my gaze to see Professor Whittlee walking beside the academy wall with his hands full. Upon seeing me, he changed course toward my direction.

"It's good to have you back. Everyone has been awaiting your return anxiously, especially the students," he said, jostling the various plant-like items in his arms. He was the academy's herbology professor, and he must have been making his way back from the greenhouse.

"Thank you, Professor," I said.

"Please, it's Quinten. I'm no longer your professor. We are colleagues now," he said with a wink and a snort-like laugh, which forced him to readjust his hold on the plants.

"Do you need some help?" I offered, extending a hand.

"No, no. I'm collecting some samples for tomorrow's class. But when I saw you in the distance, I had to make sure you were really back." Quinten was young for a professor, barely ten years my senior. The youngest on staff before Alon gave me his old position. "The students will be so glad to see you back. Their combat training hasn't been the same in your absence. Not to say that Professor Routledge hasn't done a fine job," he added quickly, his cheeks already darkening.

"Don't worry," I said, lifting the corner of my mouth. "I know Professor Routledge did more than an adequate job in my absence. But thank you, it's good to be back." No matter how long it lasts...

"I best be off. Got to go take care of these beauties." He raised his shoulders, showing the collection in his arms.

"Good night, Profess...Quinten," I corrected upon his lowered gaze. He gave me a bright grin before heading back toward the academy.

I took another deep breath and lifted my eyes to the top turrets of the academy. The reality of what was about to happen made the air around me feel heavy. I continued toward the building. There were a few things I wanted to check before joining everyone for dinner. Rolling my shoulders, I mentally prepared for what would follow next. However, there was one thing none of us could prepare for. Talia's reaction to the truth.

Chapter 10

Talia

I PRESSED MY BACK into the chair, playing with the fingernail on my thumb as I scanned the room, trying not to notice the sets of eyes on me. Multiple pedestals lined the wall. Each with vases filled with vibrant flowers sitting on top of them, bringing some warmth to the room, since there was no natural light. Overall, the decoration was minimal. The large table we were seated at occupied most of the space. I paused my tour of the room at the double doors across from me—my escape.

The doors burst open. I jumped, and every head turned to watch Raph make his way to the empty seat next to Adira and directly across from me.

"Thank you for joining us," Alon addressed Raph with a tight expression from his seat. "Now that we are all here, I guess some introductions are in order."

Adira leaned over and whispered something in Raph's ear, giving him a worried look. He shook his head and gave a clipped response before giving his full attention to Alon. Something was wrong. From his disheveled appearance and how he entered the room, it wasn't that hard to tell.

His gaze flicked to me, and his eyes narrowed as if trying to read me. I pulled back at the same time Alon said, "The only people you don't know here are Richard and Hanna Debrois." Alon gestured toward the couple sitting to the left of him, sandwiched between him and Raph. It was obvious that the couple were Gil and Adira's parents, with their matching platinum blonde hair and fair skin. "They are equivalent to what you know as village Elders. They make sure everything is running smoothly in Aydencia."

"It's an honor to meet you." Richard inclined his head toward me. Hanna, meanwhile, stared at me with misty eyes.

"It's a pleasure to meet you both," I said, flicking my gaze to the doors again. "I am grateful you allowed me to come to your secret...village." I pressed my lips together trying to figure out the best way to say what was really on my mind.

Richard gave his wife a slight nudge, startling her.

"My dear," Hanna's voice was sweet and light, "you will always be welcome in Aydencia." She continued to stare with this certain sadness in her eyes.

I wiped my hands on my pants, trying to dry the sweat as everyone's focus stayed on me.

"No reason to let the food get cold. We will discuss things after dinner," Richard said, patting his wife's hand.

Everyone lifted silver lids off the enormous platters in the middle of the table, and the smell of herbs and spices wafted out. My stomach growled in anticipation of finally eating real, fresh food again. The rations on the knarve were stale bread and salted meat, not the most appetizing.

We sat at a large rectangular table, and everyone took turns passing the food around. Eitan, who sat on my right, passed me a bowl of crispy potatoes smothered in butter and different seasonings. I took two spoonfuls before I passed them onto Hafsa.

My attention was drawn as I felt Raph's fiery stare on me again. I ignored him, confused about what I had done now to have him so focused on me. He shouldn't be concerned anymore. I was finally right where he wanted me.

"So, what is Aydencia?" I asked no one in particular, mostly to break the heavy silence and to build the courage to ask when I could leave. Everyone looked at me with confused expressions. "I mean...well, I've never heard of it before. Do you consider it to be a kingdom separate from Landore?"

"I'm sure finding out that there is a whole city hidden away was quite a shock." Richard lowered his utensils and wiped his mouth with a napkin. He glanced at Alon, who gave him a slight nod of his head. "When Madden staged his royal coup and successfully stormed the palace with his followers, killing the royal family—"

"You know that King Madden killed the royal family?" I leaned forward, thinking of the queen's journal. I had planned to tell Alon about it when we had a moment alone, but the news about my parents had thrown me. I didn't even recall how I ascended the mountain to get to this building in the first place.

"Of course," he said without hesitation.

"Then how can he still be on the throne? Why haven't you told all of Landore about this?" I looked around the table to pitying faces. They knew. My gaze stopped on Raph for a moment. His intense stare hadn't changed from earlier, but now he seemed intrigued, like he was waiting to see what I would do next.

"Fear is a powerful motivator. It can also act as blinders," Alon explained.

I lifted my brow at him.

"Madden was able to sway many of the king's inner circle to his side, promising comforts and riches if they followed him. And if they didn't, he showed them exactly how short their lives would be."

I swallowed hard. My hand shook when I reached for my glass, struggling to fight back the memories of the things I had seen King Madden do.

"Many who remained loyal to King Davis and Queen Aleese fled for their lives," Richard continued. "Not wanting to stay and serve that usurper but not wanting to die either. There were around thirty of us then. We were kids..." He smiled softly at Hanna. "Both of our parents were on King Davis's council and Alon's father was captain of the king's Royal Guard."

My eyes widened. And when I went to question Alon, I found I wasn't the only one shocked by this information. Adira, Eitan, and Raph were each looking at one another. Adira leaned forward, about to ask her own questions when her father cut in.

"I thought it was time," Richard said to Alon as he dipped his head in almost a submissive way.

"You're correct. It is time for all secrets to be told." Alon's eyes flicked to me. My breath caught in my lungs.

Hafsa found my hand under the table and gave it a little squeeze, startling me.

Alon pushed his plate forward. "From what Raph has told me, it seems you know already that you are Talia Breon, Princess of Landore."

I bit the inside of my cheek, holding back my grimace. I knew they would find out sooner or later that King Madden announced I was the granddaughter of the late king and queen. However, I wasn't ready for the change that knowledge would bring.

"Raph delivered the report on the mission," Alon explained. "Adira. Eitan," Alon dipped his head in their direction, "congratulations on a successful mission, bringing the lost princess home safely."

Home. This wasn't my home. My home was burned to the ground. Wait, my mind finally took in the entirety of what he said. Were they only in Llycia to find the lost princess and bring her back to Aydencia? I had assumed they were there to save the kidnapped young women. If they hadn't found out that it was me, would they have even tried to rescue me? My eyes slid to Raph. Was he only worried about my safety because it was part of the mission? My chest tightened. Too many questions were running through my head, and my chest felt like it was about to explode.

"I'm not the lost princess," I blurted. Everyone's face went slack. "It was a ruse by King Madden. He told me days before the wedding that he picked me to be the 'lost princess' because of my appearance alone. That he could just as easily find someone else to play the late queen's granddaughter." No one moved. "I'm sorry," I said with an exhale, "but I'm not your lost princess." The pressure that had been building inside of me released and the hope that I could get rid of this notion of being a princess started to build.

"Of course you are! You look just like them!" Hanna's voice was tight, and this time a tear escaped her misty eyes. "When I first saw you, I thought my eyes were playing tricks on me. She looks so much like Adeline, doesn't she, Richard?"

"Yes, except her nose. That is definitely Jaxon's nose." Richard's eyes grew misty, matching Hanna's.

"Who's Jaxon?" I asked.

"He's your father. Jaxon and Princess Adeline were your parents and our best friends." Hearing their names made my breaths shallow. Emotions I had buried deep down started to rise, but I shoved them down again.

"No, my parents are John and Laurel. And I plan to find them as soon as possible." I looked at Alon. It was getting hard to breathe.

"Of course." Hanna placed a hand over her heart. "I was only referring to your birth parents."

"But they're not my birth parents!" I said, placing both of my hands on the table. Hanna's gaze dropped to her lap.

"You can't believe whatever Madden told you when you were with him," Richard said, resting his hand on Hanna's shoulder.

"Richard's right," Alon interjected. "Everything Madden said was to progress his agenda. He was manipulating you."

"But where's the proof? Sure, I look like the late queen, but even you two," I pointed to Hanna and Richard, "have similar features to me. Regardless, my *actual parents* are missing. All I can focus on right now is finding them."

"And I promise you, we will do all that we can to find them and ensure their safety." Alon leaned forward. "But in the meantime, will you try to hear what we have to say, I truly believe Princess Adeline and Jaxon were your...well, birth parents." He waited for me to react again.

My priority was finding my parents, not figuring out if I was truly this lost princess or not, but it would be easier if I had their help. I gave a curt nod, which brought about a release of tension in the room. Even Hafsa and Nadav seemed to relax a little more in their seats.

Alon released a breath. "When Madden and his men took over the palace, my father ordered me to protect the royal children. I failed at saving Prince Stephen and Prince George, but I reached Princess Adeline in time." Alon's voice was low, and his gaze lowered. "We escaped with a handful of others," his gaze flicked to Richard and

Hanna, "and that's when we started bouncing from one place to the next—"

"Many whose origins were from the other kingdoms, like us, weren't welcomed anymore," Richard cut in. "With rumors circulating about one of the other kingdoms having killed the royal family, we had to go into hiding." My thoughts went to the safe house we had spent the night in. "We tried to sail to our neighboring allies." He gave a glance over to Nadav and Hafsa, who returned it with a tight smile. "But since the peace treaty never got signed, every kingdom closed their borders, fearing a war might start. We traveled around Landore, never staying in one place too long, hiding from Madden and his guards. But our group continued to grow, and we had a close call one day." His eyes flicked to Alon. "We ended up sailing north hoping we would find some piece of land to find refuge on."

"We honestly don't know how we came upon the hidden entrance in the mountains, unless someone was watching out for us and guiding our way," Hanna chimed in. "Going through the canal, we stumbled upon this abundant piece of land. This haven. And during that time Princess Adeline met Jaxon. They fell madly in love with each other. They were over the moon when they found out she was expecting." She gave me a smile that could only be described as motherly. But there were too many conflicting emotions inside of me to receive it.

I wanted them to stop calling these two strangers my parents, yet I couldn't deny the curiosity I had about their story. "They loved you more than life itself, but they were also terrified for your future. And one day they both just..." She pressed her lips together with a shake of her head.

"They disappeared," Richard finished, placing his hand over Hanna's. "None of us knew what happened or where they went until a month later when we received correspondence from the Kingdom of Vasdere saying they never made it. We realized that they had tried to flee to protect you and give you a life free from Madden." I fidgeted in my seat at Richard's words and intense stare. "But along the way, they must have gotten caught by the King's Guard. We thought the three of you were dead."

A heavy silence lingered. I couldn't stop my legs from trembling.

"Until you found us in the woods near Gasmere," Alon said with a slight upturn of his mouth.

"Wait." My jaw dropped. "Did you believe me to be the lost princess from the moment you saw me? Is that why you let me come with you so easily?" The unease inside me quickly turned to anger.

"Yes." His expression resembled an apology, but I couldn't forgive him. He lied to me. They all did. I looked at Raph, Adira, and Eitan, feeling foolish and betrayed. I couldn't take any more of this. It was all too much.

I stood. "I need some time." Then I pushed back my chair and raced from the room. I followed the hallway until I came to the front door. Desperately needing some fresh air, I opened it and ran.

CHAPTER 11

Talia

Using the shadows as a cover, I followed the paths and bridges leading down the mountain, distancing myself from everything that happened. How could I trust anything they had told me? It could all be one giant lie to get me to stay and become *their* lost princess.

Laughter filled the air. Losing my footing, I stumbled down a few steps, attracting the attention of a group of children playing in front of a house nestled partially into the mountain on my left. Their stares were enough to remind me I was an outsider. A stranger. I lowered my head and pressed on.

Some clothing hanging out to dry blew in the wind, catching my attention. I didn't have a plan or know where to go, but I knew I needed to stay unnoticed. I wrapped a cloak around my shoulders. The fabric provided a sense of security amid my out-of-control emotions. It didn't matter if what they told me was true. It didn't change the fact that my parents were missing and King Madden would most likely be looking for them. The scent of freshly baked bread wafted through the air and mingled with the distant sounds of music and chatter. With the cloak shielding me from prying eyes, I continued down the pathway, careful to keep my hood up and blend in with the locals. I didn't stop, not until I reached the end of the wooden pier.

I raised my eyes to the darkened sky and wrapped my arms around myself.

None of this was what I wanted. I was supposed to find my parents and then together we would find somewhere safe to build a new life. I released my arms from my waist. I felt trapped. Not only within this hidden city but inside of my body. Again, I was a prisoner and helpless. Everything inside of me wanted to break out, to be released. The sense of urgency grew stronger; telling me exactly what I had to do.

I peered over my shoulder to the nearby knarves tied to the different docks. Snuggled in the middle of them was a smaller one that differed from the others. My gaze then flicked to the passageway we had come through. Not allowing myself to overthink anything, I made my way to the smaller vessel, thankful the villagers seemed to be in their homes for the night.

The moment my feet landed on the boat, I held my breath to take in the subtle rocking beneath me and the sight of the ropes and sails. "I can do this," I whispered, taking a deep breath and gathering my resolve. It was time to find my parents.

With new determination, I approached the ropes that secured the boat to the dock and tried to make quick work of untying them. I wrestled with the stubborn knot, annoyed by Raph's refusal to allow me to help more when we had been at sea. As I unsheathed the dagger he had given me, a solitary tear trickled down my cheek, its warmth contrasting with the coldness of the hilt. My parents were out there somewhere. I had to do this. The urgency within me grew stronger as the thick rope strained against my rigid movements. But I sawed through it, the sound echoing through the air.

"How far did you think you'd get?"

With a sudden jerk backward, the dagger slipped from my grasp and landed on the floor with a loud clang. Raph stood near the side of the boat with his arms crossed tightly over his chest and an obvious expression of annoyance on his face that matched how I felt.

I picked up my dagger and pointed it at him. "I'm not staying here. I'm going to find my parents."

The side of his mouth lifted as he stalked toward me. "And is *that* supposed to prevent me from stopping you?" he asked, eyeing the dagger.

Despite my hand shaking, I refused to lower it. "I'm serious," I said, pushing the dagger forward. "I can't stay. I refuse to be used by all of you so you can have your lost princess." My breathing was erratic. "So, you can either help me leave or get off."

Lifting my chin, I widened my stance as he continued to advance. His unrelenting stare and long strides caused my stomach to tighten. He was an arm's length away. I shuffled back, keeping the same distance between us until my back pressed against a solid object.

"Are you really going to use my own dagger against me?" he asked, a flicker of amusement dancing in his eyes.

"If I have to," I said in a lowered voice. He leaned forward. The tip of the dagger pressed against his chest, but his focus stayed fixed on me. My whole body was on fire and for a moment I forgot why I was so upset.

"It's your move, Princess."

Throwing the dagger at his feet, I pushed him back with the palms of my hands. "I can't do this anymore!"

"Do what?" His eyes widened, but he allowed the force to create distance between us.

"I..." I wanted to say this dance we kept doing with each other. To demand he tell me if he had any feelings toward me. "I...I won't be a prisoner again." I couldn't risk knowing the truth.

"You aren't," he replied with obvious confusion.

"Right," I said, flicking my gaze to the sky. "So you're not here to stop me?"

"Yes, but that's not because you're a prisoner. It's not safe for you out there. We are trying to protect you."

"How am I to believe that after finding out you have all been lying to me since the moment we met?" I gestured toward the top of the mountain. "Maybe I don't want your protection," I said, taking a step toward him. "I'm tired. I'm tired of all of this." I threw my hands in the air. "I'm not a princess and I don't care to be one. All I care about is finding my parents."

Raph's jaw tightened, but he said nothing right away. I wouldn't take it back because it was the truth, and it was time I stopped letting others tell me what to do.

"I understand."

My jaw dropped. "You're going to let me go?"

"No," he said with a shake of his head. "You can't sail this." I crossed my arms but didn't argue. "But I'll make you a deal."

I lifted a brow.

"Give Alon a week to find out about your parents. After that week, if he has found nothing, you are free to leave. I will even escort you back to Gasmere or wherever you planned to go," he said with a smirk as he looked out toward the opening in the mountains.

I wasn't amused by his lack of faith in me, but I knew he was right. I wouldn't have made it far sailing on my own, and if my parents were still with one of theirs, Alon would be the first one to know their location. "That's it?" There had to be more to the deal.

"During that week, you need to cooperate and not fight back. Listen to what Alon has to say and consider that you could be the lost princess."

I snorted with a slight shake of my head. This was all too familiar.

"Do we have a deal?" he asked, extending his hand.

I walked forward. "How do I know you won't go back on your word?"

His gaze intensified. "You'll have to trust me," he said, continuing to hold his hand out.

I wanted to believe I didn't, but deep down I knew I trusted him more than I should. "It's a deal," I said, grabbing his hand. My stomach tightened from the warmth running up my arm.

As I tried to pull away he held on. "The three of us didn't know who you were until the night of the ball when Madden announced you," he said, releasing my hand and turning away.

Chapter 12

Jules

"WE NEED TO MOVE people out," my father said, speaking over the other Elders in the room. "We are running out of resources."

"Where are they supposed to go?" Agatha, one of the Farmers' Elders asked. The Elders around the table focused on her. Their faces showed the exhaustion they felt from discussing what to do for the past hour. "We have already heard reports that many villages are turning our people away."

"They're scared," Joan whispered, picking at the sleeve of her yellow tunic.

"Rightfully so. Who's to say what happened to Gasmere couldn't happen to them?" Agatha stood, taking time to look at everyone in the small room, even the handful of us witnessing the meeting from the side.

It was a miracle that the Meeting House hadn't been burned to the ground. It was the only building that was still fully intact and every space inside, save this room, was being used as a shelter for those with young children and the elderly. My back straightened against the wall as her gaze stayed on me. "And who knows what those rebels are capable of?"

I matched her targeted stare. I wasn't threatened by her implication that I was associated with the rebels. If it was up to me, I would have announced to the whole village the truth about the so-called rebels.

"What do you suggest we do, Agatha?" my mother asked, giving me a pointed look. She and Father were against us saying anything just yet. "It's been a week since the fires. The ground is freezing and the temperature continues to drop every day."

"The only way any of this will stop is when either the rebels or the King's Guard find what they are looking for," Agatha answered with a small lift of her lips.

"What are you saying?" Cyrus chimed in. He had been silent so far, staring at the other Healer seat beside him. They were holding off on replacing Talia's mother, even if *some* were pushing for it to happen.

"I'm suggesting we send out a hunting party to find the person responsible for all of this in the first place and give her back to the king." Agatha sat back in her seat. I clenched my fists even though the thought that Agatha wasn't entirely wrong crossed my mind. I snuffed it out, already feeling guilty. "Or we find her parents, who just happened to disappear a fortnight ago, telling no one." She gave a sharp look at my parents.

"I volunteer to lead the hunting party." Jacob Martin spoke from the far wall, his crimson uniform declaring where his alliance truly lay.

I took a step forward to speak my mind. How he played a part in this. Tals informed me that he was the one who informed the King's Guard of our return, leading to her being taken. If he hadn't, none of this would have happened. My father stood, giving me a look before addressing Jacob.

"We have not decided on anything yet. And for those we have welcomed into this meeting, please remember you are here to observe and be a witness, that is it," he finished and sat back in his chair.

The other observers shuffled along the walls. I'd been surprised when my parents asked me to attend. I'd been begging them to attend one of these since I was a little girl. But now, with Luc's gaze fixed on me, I couldn't help but question their motives.

He stood with his back firmly pressed against the wall. He was almost a head taller than me, and his loose-fitting tunic did nothing to hide his wide muscular frame. His intense stare was highlighted by his short, ash-brown hair. Many young women in our calling found him attractive and were jealous of the attention he showed me, but I never trusted his intentions.

His father's early passing had garnered my parents' sympathy. Despite Luc being two years older than me, my father had entrusted him with most of the training for new Hunters. It was clear what their expectations were for our future. But Luc's interest in me lay solely in the idea of becoming the next head Elder of Gasmere like my parents. I was a means to and end to him. I clenched my jaw and stared forward.

"We must reach a conclusion," Cyrus spoke after a long pause.

"I agree. We have run out of room here and there are still many with no shelter," Josef said, looking to Tren, his fellow Merchant Elder.

"My vote is with Elder Agatha," Derek announced. I had to catch myself from rolling my eyes. Of course her lackey would side with her.

My father massaged the bridge of his nose. "We are not taking votes yet."

"Why not? We only have two options. Either send our people out into the wild, which for those not of age, it is against the law—"

"Surely, King Madden would understand." Joan stopped fiddling with her yellow tunic to grab her fellow Elder and husband's hand.

"Is it worth the risk? To lose your children to the king? To never see them again?" Agatha looked at Joan and then to the others in the room who had children underage.

I ground my teeth. She was manipulating them.

"If they stay here, they might not survive the winter," my mother countered.

My father, meanwhile, looked around the room at each Elder. His gaze landed on Jacob and his lips pressed into a straight line. "I propose we take one more day to consider what is truly at stake and reconvene tomorrow for a vote."

Everyone around the table nodded their heads in agreement.

"One day will not change the law or my mind." Agatha stood and placed her hands on her hips. "But if that is what you all need to see the truth, then fine." She turned on her heels and walked straight out the door. Elder Derek and Jacob followed behind.

Everyone slowly rose. My father gave my mother a pointed look and then quickly found Cyrus. My mother turned to speak to Joan in a lowered voice, so I made my way out of the room.

Small cots lined the walls of the hallway, creating a narrow path to navigate as a barely tolerable stench of body odor filled the air. Leaning over the end of a cot, a mother sat on the floor, keeping a watchful eye on her two sleeping children. Her hand gently brushed through the hair of one of them as tears slid down her cheeks.

I shook my head. Something needed to be done.

"It's not right." Luc stopped next to me.

I pressed my lips together and lowered my head, trying to swallow the lump in my throat and not removing my gaze from the two sleeping children.

"Something doesn't add up about those rebels…"

I turned my head to look him in the eye. "What do you mean?" I felt my stomach constrict.

"I'm smarter than you give me credit for." The side of his mouth lifted, giving him a playful look. He had never been shy about his interest in me. "I know it's not a coincidence that the same day the crown prince and the King's Guard come into town is also the same day you return with some stranger." Luc leaned closer and I pulled back. "What have you been up to?"

"Jules, are you ready?" my mother called out.

My parents were standing by the door waiting for me. I gave them a nod. "See you later, Luc," I said, turning away. I could feel his eyes on me as I followed my parents out of the Meeting House.

The Penta was full of villagers, which was unsurprising since everyone knew that the Elders were holding a meeting that morning. My parents squared their shoulders as they made their way into the expectant crowd.

"Has a decision been made?" a Merchant was bold enough to ask.

"What are we going to do about food?" someone else yelled from the crowd.

My father cleared his throat. "We will have a formalized plan to share with everyone tomorrow." His voice didn't carry to the entire crowd as it usually could, but people passed on his message quickly. Grumbles carried through the air, but no one else said anything.

We made our way through the Penta when a spot of red caught my eye. Jacob Martin was headed toward a group of the King's Guard. After Prince Kasper left, a handful of guards stayed behind. They did little besides watch from the sidelines. It was clear they weren't here to help rebuild. I mashed my lips together as I glared at the back of Jacob's head.

"Jules," my mother called from ahead.

I turned to follow. We said nothing to each other until we reached the Hunter's quarter.

"Okay, what do you two have planned?" I asked. I knew my parents. And that look my father gave Mother after the meeting was no ordinary look. They were planning something.

"Later," she whispered over her shoulder.

I bit my tongue.

Our quarter looked like the others, homes reduced to ash and debris scattered everywhere. The canvas tents that had been set up for temporary shelter came into view. However, their thin material offered little protection against the dropping temperatures.

We arrived at our tent, the smallest one, but it meant we were fortunate to have the benefit of not having to share with another family. The other tents accommodated two to three families, but it still wasn't enough for the whole quarter.

I was last to enter. "Will you tell me what is going on?"

"I take it that the meeting didn't go too well?" Gil asked. He was in the middle of the tent at a table, folding food packages for families. It was deemed best that he stay hidden to not raise suspicion from the King's Guard or the villagers, but I guess word had traveled about him.

"Son, would you mind if we cleared off a bit of this table?" Father asked, placing a hand on Gil's shoulder. It hadn't taken but an hour after I returned home with a strange man for Gil to charm both of my parents. He had them wrapped around his finger, especially after we explained what had transpired in Llycia in the past few weeks.

"Of course not. What can I do to help?" Gil moved the completed packages into a pile on the floor.

"Eliza, do you have the map?" my father asked.

"Right here." She came over, spreading out a familiar map onto the table. It was the same one that had been sprawled out on the Caffrey's table when Tals and I returned. My breath hitched as I stepped forward and the red marks over the different villages came into view. My mind flashed through the faces of the different young women from those villages. The three of them peered over the map unaware of the sudden anxiety coursing through me as I relived my time in that wagon with the others.

"So, they agreed to move the women, children, and elderly?" Gil asked.

"Not entirely," my father answered.

"What are we going to do? We must do something." I forced my mind to focus on the problem at hand.

"Your mother and I believe every family should decide for themselves. No one should have the decision forced upon them to leave or stay."

"I agree." Gil nodded while staring at the map as though it could give him the answer we needed.

"But Elder Agatha will never go for that. And Jacob would probably run and tell the moment anyone underage left," I said.

"Yes. That is why we must spread the word and start moving people out tonight," Father stated.

"Tonight," I gasped.

"We have spread the word through the Hunters. Most want to leave, and we told the Elders who would be most compliant to do the same. Each calling will meet outside our quarter in the forest at dusk."

I ran a hand through my hair. Everything was moving so fast. There were too many unknown variables.

"But where are they going, and who is going to lead them? Elder Agatha will find out." I looked between my parents, wondering if they truly had thought this through.

"Yes, she will. But she won't know where everyone is going. Your mother and I will deal with her and Jacob."

"We will ask for volunteers to help lead. As Elders we must stay behind," my mother finished.

"I volunteer to help lead a group," I blurted.

"We imagined so," my father said. His face pulled tight, but his eyes seemed to smile.

"I'll go with Jules," Gil said.

I fought to not roll my eyes when my mother gave my father a knowing glance. They didn't understand that Gil had promised to look after me for Tals, there was nothing more to him volunteering.

"We would be extremely grateful," my mother said to Gil.

"I also volunteer." The flap of our tent opened, and Luc stepped through it.

"Luc," my father said with a bow of his head, clearly not even a little surprised by his appearance. "Your tracking skills would be a great asset to any of the groups."

Luc returned the gesture and then fixed his gaze on me. "I would like to accompany Jules."

Heat flared in my cheeks as Gil stepped next to me. "I will already be *accompanying* her."

"And *who* exactly are you?" Luc asked, stepping closer and giving Gil a once-over.

I stepped away from them. The last thing I needed were two overbearing men trying to stake their claim.

"Luc, this is Gil," my mother said with a suppressed smile. "He helped bring Jules back home safely and has graciously offered to help the village in any way he can."

"And how long will that be for?" Luc asked, not removing his eyes from Gil.

"Let's just say I'm in no rush to leave." Gil positioned himself even closer to me.

I moved forward and looked down at the map. "Where are we going?" I asked.

Luc matched my posture on the other side of me. "We have heard some reports that the villages to the west have refused to take anyone in."

I looked at my father, and he gave a reluctant nod.

"If I may," Gil started, coming to the other side of me. "In my travels I stayed some time at the village of Hattlee, and still have a few friends there that I believe would help."

Tals told me about their time in Hattlee, and it would probably be our best shot. "I agree with Gil. That would be the best place to start."

Luc's shoulders tensed as he took a sharp inhale.

"It's settled then," my father said, rolling up the map. "You three will help lead a group of those willing to leave for Hattlee."

"Ready for another adventure?" Gil said, giving me one of his signature winks.

Luc came and placed his arm around my shoulder, which I ducked out of.

"I'm going to get some air," I said. They both stepped forward. "Alone." I walked straight out of the tent but still caught my mother's stifled laughter.

Releasing an exhale, I marched straight for the trees.

CHAPTER 13

Talia

As I woke, I had to remind myself of my current situation and the uncertainty that lay before me. I buried my face in the covers and let out an audible groan of protest.

"Finally, you're up."

My scream filled the room as I launched myself off the bed. Adira placed the book she had been reading on her lap with a faint smile on her face. She sat next to the unlit fireplace.

"Don't you know it's bad luck to scare someone first thing in the morning," I said, clenching my chest.

"You might be interested to know that it's not morning. You just missed the midday meal."

"What?" I looked out the window next to the bed for confirmation. The sun was already past its peak. I guess my body was still trying to recover.

"And I will not let you spend another day holed up in this room." She scrunched her nose while uncrossing her legs and standing from the chair.

The whole point of me hiding in the small room was to try to sort out everything, along with figuring out who I could trust. The only conclusion I came to was that Adira, Eitan, and Raph hadn't lied to me. How they treated me after escaping the palace was too drastic of a change from before, plus Jules said they seemed genuinely shocked after the ball. But other than them, I didn't know who I could trust out there.

"I don't mind," I said, crossing my arms.

Her eyes narrowed. "Alon knows about the deal you made with Raph."

"Apparently, he isn't the only one," I mumbled under my breath.

"If you don't want to come out with me and see Aydencia, that's fine, but know Alon will have other plans for you today." She waited for my answer.

A small part of me had naïvely hoped that I could get out of any princess obligations they might have for me if I waited the week out in this room. "Fine. I'll come," I said while telling myself that the small excitement I felt about seeing Aydencia was from the chance of being able to get a better layout of the area, in case I needed to escape in a week.

"Great. Here are some clothes. Freshen up and then come to the entrance hall." She threw a pile of clothes at me and headed for the door. "Oh, I snagged you some biscuits too. They're on the table," she called over her shoulder before walking out.

My priority was food. I scarfed down the two buttery biscuits near the fireplace. Then I went into the washroom and splashed some water on my face before changing into fresh clothes. Within moments, I was walking out the door.

I turned down the hall, trailing my hand across the smooth clay walls. I had done little exploring of the place, but I had noticed that only half of it was made of clay. The rest was carved out from the mountain itself, leaving a perpetual chill in the air. The building they referred to as Skyhall seemed to be some sort of meeting area like Gasmere's Meeting House, but with multiple sleeping quarters. I dropped my hand as the hallway opened into the main entrance area. Opposite me was another hallway, identical to the one I came down. Adira had mentioned it was the men's quarters when she gave me a tour the first night. To my left was a larger hallway that went deeper into the mountain. I shivered at the thought of a cave in. I couldn't understand how they lived this high up or in a mountain. It had been two nights, and I missed the forest surrounding Gasmere dearly.

"You ready?" Adira asked, leaning against the wall closest to the door.

"I think so," I said as we crossed the threshold.

We descended the mountain, for Skyhall was the highest building. Children laughing soon filled the air, and the sound of little feet followed it. Adira and I moved out of the way as a group of children rushed up the winding path.

"Slow down!" Adira yelled after them, which caused them to laugh louder. I expected to see one color of clothing on them, but that was not the case. Each of them had mixed colors on, but most wore earth tones. They continued up a different path and became hidden by a row of homes. At this height, the houses were similar to Skyhall. Parts were made of clay while the rest were carved into the face of the mountain.

"How is this possible?" I asked, taking in the surrounding homes. "How did they get the materials needed to build everything? And how could this city stay hidden for so long?" I looked at Adira.

"Those are fair questions," she said, slowing as we came to a steeper decline. "I obviously wasn't born yet when they found Aydencia, but as you heard at dinner, it was pure chance they stumbled upon it. And I don't fully know how we've stayed hidden for the past twenty-two years, but having one entrance or exit has protected us from Madden's men," she said with a shrug of her shoulders. "You saw the entrance. If you don't know what you're searching for, it's near impossible to spot."

I nodded as I followed her onto a stone bridge covered in moss.

"And for the resources," she stopped in the middle of the bridge, "they used what the land provided, but they also found out that trading between kingdoms never truly stopped."

"What do you mean?" I asked, coming beside her.

"Let's just say there are many ships out there," she threw her head in the direction of the sea, "that are still transporting goods from the different kingdoms, and our people happened to come across them."

Understanding dawned on me. They weren't isolated or even cut off like the rest of Landore. Which explained how this city could be so advanced in its architecture. Did that mean the other three kingdoms never stopped trading with one another?

"So, what do you think?" Adira asked. We were still high enough that you could see the layout of the entire city. It truly was otherworldly with the unique building designs and how the vibrant greenery contrasted against the gray of the mountain. It was different to any village I had ever seen. Below, at the base of the mountain, was a cluster of buildings where many people moved about. Further down from the buildings was the port where the ships were docked. I kept searching until I saw the entrance we had come through. Was she lying about there being one entrance or exit?

"I honestly don't know what to think. It's all a little unbelievable," I replied.

"I'm sure it's a lot to take in for the first time," she said, giving me what I assumed was a sympathetic look. Her emotions were hard to read most of the time. "We were in disbelief when we saw our first village outside of Aydencia."

"I'm sure seeing a village under the callings was strange compared to this." I gazed out, unable to deny the wonder I felt. Under different circumstances I would have loved nothing more then to hear how this place functioned without callings and to even talk with some of the locals.

"Alon had schooled us on what we could expect, but we were still in disbelief when we saw it. We didn't stop talking about the effects the segregation between callings had on the villages for two weeks straight," she said while shaking her head. "Come on, let's keep moving."

We moved down the mountain in silence, but I didn't mind. I enjoyed the chance to sort through my thoughts and scan the area. I couldn't help but contemplate a backup plan in case Raph failed to fulfill his part of the bargain. However, if there was an alternative escape route, I had no clue where to search. These mountains

were extensive and a concealed tunnel could be anywhere.

The sound of voices intensified, along with the smell
of bread and different spices. We were in the same area
as when I had attempted to escape. However, this time,
I could fully absorb my surroundings.

The street bustled with people who were engaged in
lively conversations or coming and going from the clay
buildings that lined the street. Each building had a sign
out front. One prominently displayed the word *carver*
with a picture of a wild boar. Another read *tailor*, while
a third announced its occupation as a *potter*.

Two young women caught my attention. They giggled
to one another as they emerged from the tailor's shop,
their arms overflowing with garments. I was struck by
the resemblance one of them had to Hafsa.

"Aydencia is not like other villages in Landore," Adira said, probably understanding the reason behind my
wide eyes. "You will notice that many Aydencians carry
different physical traits from the other kingdoms." She
gestured with her eyes to a young man who walked past
us. His features were light, but he had the same almond
eye shape as Nadav and Hafsa. "They didn't go into the
details at dinner, but after Madden took over, he began to hunt those who carried features from the other
kingdoms. Many tried to flee back to the kingdom their
ancestors came from, but majority never made it." My

mouth dropped open, even though I knew I shouldn't be shocked by his cruelty. "Others were lucky to find the group my parents and Alon were with, and in turn, this place." Adira extended her arms out.

"So your family's ancestry is from Vasdere?" I asked, looking at her blonde hair and remembering how surprised I was seeing her and Gil for the first time.

"They probably wanted to tell you this themselves." She lifted one side of her mouth. "They believe we are related."

"What?"

"My maternal grandmother was Queen Aleese's twin sister."

I pressed my lips together, unsure of what to say. The idea of having relatives my age was foreign to me, and I still didn't know if I believed I was Queen Aleese's granddaughter or not. "What is this area called?" I asked.

Adira dipped her head as if silently telling me she understood. "Since the callings don't rule us, everyone in Aydencia works together to produce what is needed for the village to survive. These buildings store and sell the essentials."

"Like a Penta."

"Sort of."

I stayed fixed on the women from the tailor's as they walked our way. When they caught my eye, they moved over, keeping a good distance.

"They aren't used to newcomers," she said, giving the two women a piercing look. "Many still react the same to Hafsa and Nadav."

"Why are they here? And what kingdom are they from?" I asked.

"Nefali," Adira answered partially before leading me over to a shaded area between two buildings. A small smile flitted across my lips, knowing that I had been right in my guess when I'd learned of the different kingdoms at the palace.

"And why are they here?" I asked again.

She pressed her head back against the building and released an exhale. "I'm not lying when I tell you this," she lowered her head, "but I don't know."

"How can yo—"

"They showed up almost a month before we left to help rescue the kidnapped women. But everyone has been tight-lipped on the reasoning."

"You must have some idea." I stood against the wall on the other side of her.

"We have plenty of ideas," she said with a small laugh. "Just ask my brother for some of them when you see him next. But the one that makes sense is that it is somehow connected to the lost princess." She gave me a hesitant look.

"What would Nadav and Hafsa want with Landore's lost princess?"

"Your guess is as good as mine." She pushed off the wall. "Let's keep going."

Adira let the silence drag on, and we walked toward the perimeter of the water. I glanced at the various knarves, spotting the ship I'd tried to steal as we passed by, heading toward the fields I had seen when we first entered. In the daylight it looked a lot bigger. I'd been foolish thinking I could sail it on my own. No, I would need to find someone who would help me if Raph didn't keep his word. I glanced over at Adira unsure if she would be willing to betray Alon and even her own parents.

"I thought we'd skip the port today since you already spent some time there the other night." She gave me a smirk over her shoulder.

My heart rate spiked as I wondered if she had read my thoughts. "Does everyone know I tried to escape?"

Her shoulders shook. "Basically. There's a rumor going around that a scorned young woman tried to run away from her lover."

"What!?" A flush creeped up my cheeks as I recalled Raph's intense gaze and closeness.

"Don't worry." She laughed. "No one knows it was you."

I smiled, hoping she couldn't see how uncomfortable I felt.

She led me up a grassy hill. "This is a favorite spot for Gil and me," she said, finding a seat on the ground.

I stifled a yawn as I got comfortable on the grass.

Adira shook her head at me. "Remind me to have us visit the kitchen when we get back. There is a drink Eitan's grandmother makes that will wake you right up."

I lifted my eyebrows. "Is it called coffee?"

"Yes." She leaned back with a quizzical look. "I didn't think you would have it in the villages, since it solely comes from Nefali."

"We don't. But apparently, it's King Madden's favorite drink," I explained, remembering what Celeste had told me.

"Makes sense that he would like such a bitter drink."

I nodded my head. If King Madden had access to it, did that mean he never really shut off trade with the other kingdoms? Did he only want it to seem that way?

"You see that house with the livestock?" Adira asked. I followed the direction her finger pointed, putting the whole coffee thing in the back of my mind for another time. "That's Mr. Brenner's place. Remember the story about Gil dressing up livestock in dresses?" She looked at me with raised eyebrows. I rubbed my hands through the thick grass while my thoughts went back to when they were taking Jules and me home. It felt like another lifetime. "They were his. And he still hasn't forgiven Gil." She shook her head slightly with a small upturn of her mouth.

"Do you miss him?" I asked.

She lowered herself to her forearms, looking at the blue sky. "Gil and I are different in almost every way imaginable, but we have always been each other's best friend." She paused for a moment. "This is the first time we have been away from each other, and it feels like a part of me is missing."

"I somewhat understand," I said, pulling my knees to my chest and thinking about my parents and Jules. A part of me had gone missing the day Jules was kidnapped, and I wondered if I would ever get it back. "What do Alon and your parents want with me?" I asked, dropping my chin on my knees, not expecting her to truly answer my question.

She pushed up. "I'm sorry. My parents are like village Elders, but I'm afraid I don't know the inner workings of Aydencia. However, I can tell you that since I was a young girl, I was told stories about a lost princess and how one day she would return and restore Landore to its rightful glory." She gave me a knowing look as I tried not to roll my eyes. "For many people, that is the hope they have clung to for the past thirty years. I know you might not believe that you're this lost princess, but it's more about the symbol of the lost princess and the hope she inspires."

"I can't," I said, lowering my head to the ground. "All I can worry about right now is my parents, not all of Aydencia and what they have been hoping for."

"But you have—"

"Adira!" a voice called.

CHAPTER 14

Talia

A MAN SPRINTED UP the hill. Adira jumped up and closed the distance. I pushed myself to my feet but remained an arm's length away from them.

"Your father has been looking for you," the man said, gasping for air as he tried to slow his breathing. "He needs you right away."

"Where is he?" she asked. I sensed the strain in her voice, causing my own body to tense.

"At the academy." The man straightened, pulling on the hem of his leather vest. He seemed to be wearing some sort of uniform. A tree like the one marking the entrance to Aydencia was carved into the leather over his chest. Maybe he was some sort of guard or warrior? They had mentioned there were others like them.

Adira's shoulders relaxed. "He probably wants me to cover a class for him. Tell him I'll be there soon." She waved her hand at the man, not showing any sign of concern compared to the man whose eyes darted from where he came back to her.

"He seemed adamant that I come back with you." He shifted his weight from one foot to the other.

Adira released a loud exhale. "Fine, I'll come now."

The man's demeanor switched to one of relief as he brushed some moisture off his forehead. His eyes then trailed over to me, and he lifted both eyebrows.

Adira stepped in front of me, blocking his view. "I'll be right behind you," she said to the man in a sharp tone.

Before I could ask who the man was, she spoke, "Do you think you can make it back to Skyhall by yourself?"

I peered up the mountain, where you could clearly see the lone building at the top. "No one can really miss that thing."

She followed my gaze. "True. And—"

"I promise I won't try to escape." I held up my hand. "I gave him a week."

She nodded curtly. "I'll see you at dinner," she said, descending the hill. I opened my mouth in disagreement. "Alon is expecting you to be there!" she yelled.

Releasing a sigh, I threw my head back. "Five days," I whispered, taking one more look at Skyhall before making the ascent.

About halfway up the mountain, I heard distant shouts. I told myself to let it be, but the noise came from a direction Adira hadn't shown me. What if they were hiding something from me? What if it was another way out of here? A specifically loud roar made up my mind. The commotion led me further away from the homes and onto another path into a dense section of trees. The shouts got louder. They were coming from multiple people, both men and women. Breaking through the trees, the path opened to an enormous stone building that resembled a palace. From what I could tell, the building was three levels high with hundreds of rooms. Why didn't Adira bring me here? What were they hiding?

The shouts transformed into enthusiastic cheers and guided me to the back of the palace-like building. There, I discovered a large crowd of young people in a circle. Scattered around them were an assortment of weapons and peculiar equipment that I had never seen before.

I edged closer to get a better view. No one noticed me as I made my way toward the circle. Peeking in between the crowd, I could make out two people in the middle fighting. Adrenaline coursed through my veins.

Why wasn't anyone stopping this fight? A feeling of unease settled in my gut. What type of people were the Aydencians? Not willing to stand aside while two people hurt each other, I pushed hard against the bodies until I came to the first row of spectators and froze.

Two young men were fighting in the middle, but one of them was too familiar. His brown hair clung to his forehead, drenched with sweat. My stomach tightened as I took in how his tunic hugged his body, allowing his muscles to be on full display.

They had no weapons, but their fists and legs were weapons enough. Raph circled the younger man, blocking his attacks effortlessly while barking commands. It was obvious the young man was not as experienced, and Raph was holding back. It reminded me of the time when Gil and Raph sparred in the forest. I exhaled, feeling the fear leave me instantly. They were sparring.

"Come on, Kent, show him what you can do!" A girl next to me cheered. I looked around. Everyone spectating was fairly young, and there was an air of excitement they carried as they watched to see what would happen next.

"Find an opening," Raph said to the younger man who had gone for an attack that Raph blocked. "You're running out of time."

Kent's eyes enlarged as he released a sharp breath. He danced back and forth and then approached Raph on the right before switching to the left. His right fist came around and connected with Raph's midsection, but Raph didn't react. He used the closeness to grab

Kent's other arm and spun him until it was pinned behind Kent's back. Raph kicked the back of Kent's knees, which made him fall to the ground.

Half the crowd moaned while the other half cheered louder. Raph knelt on one knee as he used his other arm to wrap around Kent's neck. It wasn't but a few moments before Kent tapped on Raph's forearm, and Raph disengaged from him.

I lowered my hand from my chest, realizing I'd been caught up in the excitement with everyone else.

Kent stayed kneeling, but Raph walked around and extended his hand. "You have gotten better since I've been gone, but you still have to watch your openings," he said, then clapped Kent on the back with a genuine smile on his face.

Kent returned to the fold of the crowd, and various people gave him words of encouragement or pats of sympathy. The group grew quiet. Pushing his hair back with his hand, Raph sauntered toward the center of the circle. I waited to see what Raph would say or do next, and I wasn't the only one. Two girls giggled in each other's ears as Raph walked past them, their eyes fixed on his every move. The sudden urge to go over there and block their view came over me. I bit my tongue instead, putting my focus back on Raph.

"Get into pairs. We will end today with sparring," Raph said. The moisture in my mouth evaporated as I watched his chest rise and fall with each breath.

Everyone moved about, which left me awkwardly standing by myself as I tried to get my brain to function properly.

All eyes moved in my direction.

"Halt," Raph ordered, locking eyes with me.

CHAPTER 15

Raph

HER BLONDE HAIR BLEW across her face, doing nothing to hide those icy-blue eyes that stared right through me. My jaw tightened. What was she doing in my class? How did she even get here? Anger rolled through me as I realized she must be alone.

"You're dismissed," I ordered. The students hesitated while gawking at her. "Now!" They quickly dispersed back into the academy. I rolled my shoulders back, knowing this would be all over the academy within the hour. "What are you doing here?" My voice felt strained as I marched toward her.

"Who are they?" she asked, her eyes dancing from me to the retreating students.

"Students. Welcome to Aydencia Academy." I gestured to the building behind me.

Her eyes widened with what seemed to be understanding as she took in its imposing height.

"You still haven't answered my question, Princess." I thought Adira was supposed to watch her? No one in Aydencia knew who she was, but people were talking about the newcomer that had returned with us. Her being out by herself was going to pique more gossip.

"If you must know," she widened her stance, "I was on a tour with Adira."

My jaw flexed. If that was true, Alon would not be happy. Talia's identity was supposed to stay a secret and parading her around Aydencia would make people ask questions, which we didn't need. "Then where is she?" I asked, scanning the empty training grounds.

"Her father requested her presence immediately."

"I still fail to see how that brought you here. Alone," I finished, furrowing my brows as the frustration built inside me. Who knows who she talked to on her way here.

She crossed her arms over her chest, showing the same strong-willed attitude as when she tried to steal the ship. "Am I not allowed to leave Skyhall?"

"No..." I searched my mind for an explanation without having to lie to her. "It's just that you're not from here. You could have easily gotten lost or even hurt."

"I'm not helpless." I didn't respond as I pictured her cutting the rope with the dagger I gave her. I fought against the upturn of my mouth as she rolled her eyes and dropped her arms. "I was heading back to Skyhall when I heard shouting. "I...", her gaze flicked to the side, "I was worried that someone was in trouble. It led me to the academy where you happened to be fighting a young student." Throwing out her chin, she continued, "So, what was all of that?"

She was an awful liar, but I wasn't going to push her for the real reason she followed the shouts. That wasn't the issue. The problem was her being left on her own. "You interrupted sparring practice. This is the combat field." I extended my hand, gesturing to the open ground around us littered with different equipment. "It's where we train the students to become the next generation of Aydencian warriors." Her eyes bulged.

"I know you said there were others like you, Adira, Gil, and Eitan, but they..." She looked in the direction the students had gone. "...are just children. And there were so many of them." She went silent for a moment, and her eyes narrowed. "Is this what Aydencia is? A place to make warriors?"

"No," I answered a little too sharply.

"Why didn't Adira show me this place? What are you hiding?" She took a step forward.

"Nothing." I squeezed my hands into fists by my side, not prepared to answer her onslaught of questions. "The Academy is much more than a place where students learn how to fight. They also learn how to read, write, and perform different trades. It was built to educate the next generation, but also to prepare them for the coming war." I winced at my slipup.

"A war?" she yelled. "You can't be serious." Her delicate hand reached for her neck, searching for the necklace she once had. A habit of hers when she needed a sense of comfort.

"Do you need to sit?" I took a step closer. Her face had gone pale. I raised my arms, afraid she was going to faint.

"I'm fine. Give me a moment." She held her hand out between us. "This war you speak of...it's to dethrone King Madden, correct?"

"Yes." I shifted my weight.

"But you can't win! He has an entire army at his disposal, and you are training kids." She gestured wildly with her arms. It was sort of cute. Quickly, I straightened and smothered that thought.

"The people of Aydencia have spent the past twenty-two years preparing for this. Trust me, we are more than ready." Her fear for the people of Aydencia was misplaced. If she knew what we were capable of and the support we had coming...

"When is this so-called war going to happen? What are you guys waiting for?" she asked, rubbing her chest.

I grabbed a water canteen nearby and took a drink, trying to buy myself some time to decide how much to tell her. "We've been waiting for the right timing."

"And is that time now?" Her eyes doubled with worry.

I remained silent, giving a noncommittal shrug. I had promised not to lie to her, but I couldn't tell her the truth. That the timeline for the war had catapulted forward the moment she stepped foot in Aydencia.

She swayed slightly and pressed her fingers against her temple. I lurched forward ready to catch her, but she was already moving toward the wooden platform we used to practice short-range fighting. She took a seat. After a few deep breaths, her gaze found me and then lowered to my chest. I followed her line of sight and realized I was completely drenched in sweat.

"There is a lot of death surrounding war," she stated, dropping her eyes to the ground. I grabbed a dry tunic on the platform. "And King Madden won't care who gets caught in the crossfires." She tightened her grip on the edge of the platform.

"I know," I said, quickly removing my wet tunic and throwing on the other one. Her eyes were glued to the ground, but a tinge of pink appeared on her cheeks. I bit my lip, suppressing the way my body reacted to her blush. I pulled myself up next to her. Warmth ignited through my whole body when my shoulder brushed against hers. I leaned away and rubbed the back of my neck. She was eerily quiet. "Are you okay?" I asked, hoping she couldn't tell how tight my voice sounded.

"Yeah." Her eyes finally left the ground and found me. "So, are you a teacher or something?"

"Yeah...something like that."

She exhaled. "Everything is always a secret with you."

I rolled my shoulders back, ignoring the pain in my chest from her words. But I couldn't let her in. "It's getting late. I should get you back."

I stood and extended my hand to help her, but she dipped her head and ignored it. She jumped off the platform and the smell of sugar and wildflowers brushed past me. I dared to lean in to have it consume me more. She continued forward, unaware of what I stole from her. I jogged to match her step. This princess was going to ruin me.

CHAPTER 16

Kasper

"HAVE YOU ALWAYS BEEN this tall?" David Colan's daughter, Jemma, asked as her eyes peered up at me. My teeth slammed together. This was the twentieth question she had asked in a row.

"No," I said, grabbing the package from the Merchant and placing it on top of the others we had picked up. I turned and almost bumped into two young women. My eyes stayed on them longer than they should have. I knew because they both blushed. One wore Merchant gray while the other wore Artist yellow.

"Excuse me," I said with a dip of my head, which sent them into a fit of giggles before scurrying away. My gaze followed them as they linked arms and dipped their heads together.

I shook my head. This village would be in trouble if my father found out callings were intermingling, and it was only a matter of time before he would. There were constant check-ins by the King's Guard with all the villages in Landore. They were done to ensure that every villager of age chose a calling and that each village stayed submissive to the king. If there was any sign of mutiny or defiance, the King's Guard were ordered to end it on the spot, by any means necessary.

Jemma's attention fixed on me. I peered down to see her with an amused smile as she looked at the two young women.

"What's left?" I asked.

Jemma pushed the dirt around with her foot, then she bowed her head and mumbled, "That was the last thing."

"Let's go." It was almost dusk and we needed to get back. I walked in the direction of the Healer's quarter, not waiting to see if she followed, because she would.

"Have you always wanted to be a Farmer?" Jemma yelled from behind me.

A moan escaped my lips. I had offered to help grab supplies for the Colans at the Penta, but that was before I knew Jemma would tag along. It was like my father had sent her specifically to torture me.

"Did you hear me?" she asked, pumping her legs as fast as she could to keep pace with me.

"Kasper!"

Julian and Oliver walked through the archway that marked the Healer's quarter behind us. I squinted against the setting sun behind them. They still wore the brown garments we had stolen, but their strides said they were anything but simple Farmers. I had sent them to go check in with Sal. Jemma bounced from one foot to the other, waving excitedly at both of them as they came closer.

"Jemma, go on without me."

"But—" she whined.

"I need to talk with Julian and Oliver." She placed her little hands on her hips and opened her mouth to say more, but I cut her off before she could argue. "Go home and set up your favorite game for us to play."

"Really?" Her face lit up like I had promised her the world.

"Yes."

"Okay, but you still have to carry those," she said, pointing to the stack of packages in my arms before running away. "And don't take forever," she yelled over her shoulder.

At the sound of muffled laughter, I turned to glare at Julian and Oliver. Their faces fell as they staggered back. Swallowing, they straightened.

"What do you have to report?" I asked.

Oliver elbowed Julian, who gave a side-eye back.

"Out with it," I commanded.

Julian shuffled forward and cleared his throat. "When we arrived, Sal and around ten of the men were gone."

"What do you mean?" I pressed my lips together while switching the packages into my other arm.

"Those who stayed back mentioned that he was tired of waiting. He took men and went to the neighboring village."

I sucked in a breath as I forced my fingers to relax around the packages. It had only been a day since we left. With all my effort channeled into remaining calm, I nodded to Julian to continue.

"We," he looked over at Oliver, "went to the neighboring village so we could report back on what Sal was up to."

"And?"

"He was rounding up villagers by calling and bringing them in for questioning," Oliver finished.

I looked past them to think. Even though Sal going off on his own, without my orders, was a sign of disrespect, at least he was distracting himself. It gave me more time to find out information here. The Colans were opening up, but I needed to move it along. We needed to move out of here quickly. Not only was Sal a threat, but if he found out where the princess or her parents were before I did...

At the sound of crackling, I relaxed my grip on the packages.

"Sir, what would you like us to do?" Oliver asked.

"Nothing right now," I said, readjusting my hold. Julian extended his arms out to take the packages, but I shook my head. "We won't be staying here much longer."

"Please, help yourself," Mrs. Colan said, placing a plate of rolls on the table next to a steaming bowl of stew.

Across the cramped table, Jemma reached for the plate of rolls first. She offered them to Julian and Oliver, who were sitting on either side of her, before taking two for herself.

"Thank you again for giving us a place to stay," I said while filling my plate.

"Oh yes, I haven't eaten this well in a long time," Julian added as he brought a spoonful of stew to his mouth.

"Why thank you." Mrs. Colan smiled fondly at him. It instantly fell the moment her gaze landed on me. No matter what I did, from the moment we met, she seemed put off by me.

I forced myself to grin, trying to seem a little more like Julian. "We won't be crowding you for much longer. We'll be moving on in a day or so."

"What!" The sound of metal hitting the table drew everyone's attention to Jemma. She had dropped her spoon and was staring at me in utter shock.

"Jemma, dear, you knew they wouldn't be staying forever," Mrs. Colan said, reaching her hand across the table to her daughter. "But you are more than welcome to stay longer if you need," she said, looking at me before darting her gaze to Julian and Oliver.

"Thank you, but it is almost time for us to go."

"It's not fair. Why does everyone always leave?" Jemma dropped her chin to her chest and started playing with the necklace that hung around her neck.

"I like your necklace," Julian whispered to Jemma, nudging her shoulder. She snapped out of her mood with a broad smile.

"My best friend Talia gave it to me, and she's—"

"Jemma," her brother interrupted, as the table bounced forward.

"Ow," Jemma cried out, reaching to her leg.

I sat straighter, fighting a genuine grin, ready to press Jemma about what she meant when Mrs. Colan jumped from her seat. "I think it's time for some pie. Marie, Mrs. Grady, dropped one off this afternoon for us." She went to fetch it even though everyone's bowls were still full of stew.

I tried to find an opening to ask more about the necklace, but Jemma dominated the conversation with her random questions about our life in Gasmere. She was especially interested in the Farmers and Healers.

"It's getting late," Mrs. Colan announced. "Jemma, it's time for bed, and Andres, you need to finish restocking the supplies."

"It's not that late," Jemma whined. But one look from her mother and she closed her mouth and pushed back her chair. "You will still be here when I get up, right?" she asked Julian.

He looked at me as if it was breaking his heart too.

"Yes, we will," I answered.

"Promise?" Jemma's big eyes zeroed in on me.

"I promise," I said in full honesty. There was no way we would leave yet, not when we had our first solid lead.

"Sorry, she's been a fiery one since the day she was born," Mr. Colan said as Jemma and Andres left the room.

"It's no problem," I said with a wave of my hand. "But her necklace reminded me of someone. Someone in Gasmere who went missing when those horrible kidnappings were happening."

Mr. Colan sat straighter. I couldn't see Mrs. Colan's face, but the dishes she had been collecting stopped clanging.

"Yes, horrible indeed." Mr. Colan's hand tremored slightly while he lifted his drink.

"I was wondering if, by some miracle, it might be the same one who gave Jemma that necklace? Her name is Talia Caffrey. We grew up with her." I gestured my head to Julian and Oliver who swallowed their food and nodded their heads in agreement.

Mr. Colan's throat bobbed up and down. "I'm afraid not. That necklace was from an old family friend."

I clung to the edge of my chair, fighting the urge to lean forward, grab the man, and demand he tell the truth as sweat formed along the ridge of his temple.

"Oh." I bowed my head in mock defeat. "I had thought maybe she might have been with that group Mr. Grady mentioned that first night we met. The ones that came and helped you?"

"Right." Mr. Colan chuckled, his smile straining.

"It's just..." I let the sides if my mouth turn down. "We've been desperate to help locate her. I know this might seem impossible to believe, but she is the lost princess."

"Oh," Mrs. Colan said as metal clanged together.

"Is that so?" Mr. Colan asked, eyeing his wife.

I tried to make my grin seem like one of those polite smiles courtiers always gave one another, and not because I had him. He showed the same signs as a prisoner about to break.

"Yes. Have you not heard about the news of the lost princess?" I asked.

"Of course." Mr. Colan shook his head as if he remembered where he had placed a lost item.

"Well, the rebels who kidnapped the princess from the palace are believed to be the same ones who torched Gasmere in search of her parents. Maybe that group who helped you might know something. Do you happen to know where they reside?"

He cleared his throat. "Truthfully, they were a group of mysterious strangers to us. They never shared where they came from or if they were even from the same village."

"What a shame. Not where they were headed?" I pried, feeling anger rise inside my chest.

He shrugged. "Maybe, north? They came from the south. But who knows where they could be," he added.

I pressed my palms into the wood of the chair and felt it crack. "Well," I released my grip with a breath. "We can only hope our travels will bring us to them."

Mr. Colan nodded.

"I think we will call it a night," I said, then turned my attention to Julian and Oliver. They both shoved the remains of their second piece of pie in their mouths.

"Of course." Mr. Colan's face relaxed. "Let us know if you all need anything."

We said good night to one another and then the three of us reentered the front of the Healing House. I walked straight to my little sectioned-off area and ignored

Julian and Oliver's curious faces. Mr. Colan confirmed what I suspected. Talia had been here with the rebels. They must have known she was the lost princess, but why had they let her go back to Gasmere? I sat on the cot, which was too small for me. None of that changed anything. I already knew she was with the rebels.

And I believed Mr. Colan didn't know their whereabouts. They wouldn't have disclosed that. I placed my head in my hands. We needed to move on from here, but something inside of me kept pulling me to stay a little longer. Like there was something I wasn't seeing.

If I found nothing new by tomorrow, we would leave. But I had one more avenue I wanted to pursue, and it had to deal with a talkative little girl.

CHAPTER 17

Talia

"Three days," I mumbled, staring out the window in my room overlooking Aydencia. I released my grip on the windowsill, walked over to the bed, and collapsed on my back with a groan. My head had not stopped spinning, thinking about the ramifications from everything Raph told me at the academy.

I had tried to keep my mind occupied over the past two days by doing things, but I wasn't allowed outside anymore, not after Alon found out Adira took me on a tour of the city without his approval. He asked if I would wait until they figured out a way to inform the people about my presence, which in light of the deal I made with Raph, I agreed. So, I had two options: stay in this room all day, which at least had a window, or explore Skyhall. But I still refused to go too deep into the mountain, for fear of it collapsing on me.

Eitan and Adira tried their best to entertain me, but they had their own responsibilities. Eitan let me help him out in the kitchen once, but when his grandmother spotted me, she quickly ushered me out, saying it was no place for a princess.

The sound of knocking filled the room. I didn't bother moving. The door creaked open, and I lifted my head to drop it again as I saw Adira.

"What's that?" I asked, referring to the box she had in her hands.

"Something you're going to hate," she said. Her footsteps stopped and were replaced with the sound of her setting the box on the table.

I rolled over onto my side and lifted my eyebrows. Adira stood by the box, but she wasn't in her usual all black. Instead, she fidgeted with a brown leather vest. The tunic underneath was blue, but the vest covered most of it, along with the matching leather shoulder and wrist cuffs. Her entire outfit resembled one of a warrior.

"What's going on?" I felt my throat constrict.

"Alon has organized a dinner this evening."

My shoulders relaxed. "And?"

"And he expects you to be present as Princess Talia, per the deal."

I blew out an audible breath as I fell back on the bed. "Let me guess, inside the box is what I'm supposed to wear?"

She paused. "It's a dress."

"I figured."

This felt too familiar. But I knew it was only a matter of time before Alon would request me to play the part of the lost princess. I was just hoping news of my parents would come first.

"You okay?" she asked, walking closer to me.

"Yeah." I forced myself to sit up. "What's the purpose of the dinner?" I asked, lifting my chin toward the box.

"It's nothing huge. There are a couple of influential people of Aydencia that Alon would like you to meet." Her tense posture told me there was something else to it.

"Right," I said, approaching the box.

Adira didn't respond or convey any more about the dinner. Our friendship had changed since they rescued me from King Madden. She didn't see me as just Talia anymore.

I lifted the lid of the box, in which an emerald dress lay folded. Picking it up, I headed for the washroom, not caring what the dress actually looked like. A dress was a dress at this point. A costume to go with the role-playing.

"I'll be ready shortly," I said before closing the door.

At least Adira hadn't lied to me. There were only four faces seated at the table that were unfamiliar. Despite it being a smaller gathering, my stomach churned with nerves from the moment I stepped into the dining hall. Everyone was dressed as if they were ready for a royal occasion or a war. Raph and Eitan had on similar leather outfits to Adira, and the three of them sat further down at the table.

"Welcome everyone." Richard stood from the head of the table. He wore a fancy jacket that was short in the front and longer in the back.

I was surprised not to see Alon sitting at the head, but he took a seat to the right of Hanna at the other end of the table. He wore a leather outfit, similar to the other three, but he had markings covering his right chest plate.

"We shall start with some introductions before we partake in the delicious meal before us." Richard gestured to the platters scattered across the long rectangular table. Meats, roasted to perfection, filled most of them while vibrant and crisp vegetables surrounded them. The table also had an assortment of breads that were shaped into unique designs. "First, I would like to introduce a very honored guest." Every eye turned to me. "Princess Talia Breon of Landore, the lost princess." Richard gestured toward me with an open palm. I squirmed in my seat and tried to give my best smile.

I tried to pay attention to the names and titles he spouted next, but they were foreign to me. What intrigued me more was watching how Raph, Adira, and Eitan responded to their introductions. They each bowed their heads to the person being introduced and looked at them with an intense gaze.

From what I could conclude, the woman sitting across from me and to the left of Richard, was in charge of Aydencia's fleet of knarves. She was the only other one wearing that leather uniform. Everyone else looked as if they were ready to attend a ball, even Nadav and Hafsa. The older man sitting to the right of me dealt with the wealth of Aydencia, and the two other men who were at the other end had something to do with their laws and relaying information to the people.

"I'm sure I speak for everyone when I say we have been waiting for this day to come for most of our lives. And now it's here. So, let's celebrate!" Richard grabbed the chalice in front of him and held it up. Everyone followed in response. I grabbed mine as well. "To the lost princess," he said, extending it in my direction.

"To the lost princess," everyone echoed, then took a drink in unison. I set my chalice down without tasting it.

The food was passed around the table, once Richard had taken his seat. The older man to my right bowed his head with a wide grin when I passed him a platter filled with small, round balls made of meat. I grimaced back, unable to fake a genuine smile.

"Princess Talia," one man on the other end called out, breaking the prolonged tension in the room. He wore a jacket like Richard's, but it barely covered his stomach, showing the tightness of his undershirt. "What do you think of Aydencia so far?"

I cleared my throat. "Well...I've only had one official outing so far." I flicked my gaze to Adira. "But it's definitely intriguing."

"Richard," the man said, leaning back in his chair. "We must fix this."

"We will." Richard shared a look with Alon. "Once we have figured out a way to notify the people of her presence."

"Ah yes, we must do that in the right way," the man sitting across from the other one spoke. He was younger but reminded me of the noblemen from the palace because of how he carried himself. "There are already rumors circulating, and we want to do it in a way that will most benefit the cause and stir up hope." He rubbed his chin.

I stopped chewing.

"What about a ball?" the man with the tight jacket offered.

The man sitting next to me spoke, "I don't think that would be the best decision for Aydencia with what will come next."

I swallowed and opened my mouth to remind them that this all hinged on if they heard news of my parents in the next three days.

"What about a coronation?" The larger man tried again.

"We should give the people time to know her first, don't you think?" The woman across from me looked at the younger man.

"Most definitely. A public tour of the city would create a way for the people to see her close and in person. What do you think of a public tour, Your Highness?"

I started to speak, but Alon cut me off.

"We can discuss this later," he said, giving Richard a pointed look before switching his attention to me.

I tightened my grip around the fork in my hand.

"Yes, you are quite right, Alon. This doesn't have to be decided now," Richard said with a forced smile.

"Yes." I stabbed a piece of food with my fork. "Especially if I end up leaving in three days," I said, sliding my teeth against the metal.

The room fell silent. I forced myself to keep chewing as everyone stared at me. A forced laugh broke out.

Richard looked down the table at his wife, who followed his laugh with her own. Soon, the room broke out with forced laughter.

"Her Highness is joking," Richard said.

"I am not." I set my fork down with a clang. "You are all talking as if I have already agreed to become your princess, but that's not the case." I looked straight at Alon. "The deal was that I would give you a week to find my parents, and if you failed, I could leave Aydencia to look for them myself. That deal expires in three days."

Alon's expression remained unreadable. From the corner of my eye, I could tell Raph was giving me a heated stare, but I didn't care.

"Excuse me, Your Highness, but your parents are dead," the larger man said in a softer tone.

Fear strangled my heart, choking the breath from my lungs.

"She is referring to the couple who took her in and raised her," Richard said to the man. I took slow breaths, trying to reassure myself they weren't talking about my real parents.

"Yes, they must be wonderful people to have taken you in," the younger man said before taking a drink from his chalice.

The man sitting next to me placed his hand closer to my plate. "They will receive compensation for their years of service to Landore."

Heat flared up my neck. "They are my parents. I am their daughter. They don't need to be compensated for anything!" I turned my glare to Richard. "I have no desire to play your lost princess."

Gasps circled the table.

"Your Highness, you are failing to understand your importance here," Richard interjected, then sending a pleading look to Alon.

"Raph already informed me of your plan to go to war against King Madden. And that you had been waiting for something," I said, looking to Alon who threw Raph a tight look. "It took little to figure out Raph was referring to the lost princess. And I'm telling you, I don't want any part in a war."

Chaos erupted.

Everyone shouted over one another, demanding answers from Richard. The only people staying quiet were Adira, Eitan, Raph, and Alon. They had their eyes fixed on me.

Bang. Bang.

Richard pounded his fist on the table. "This dinner is finished."

"You can't be serious. We need an—" The younger man closed his mouth as Richard raised his hand, halting him.

"Hanna and I will escort you out." Richard stood. "If you will," he said, gesturing with his hand.

I sat frozen as everyone slowly left their seats. Alon remained seated, his eyes zeroed in on me. He folded his hands under his chin. "We need to talk."

CHAPTER 18

Raph

I PACED OUTSIDE ALON'S study. My fingers flexed and released in frustration. We desperately needed to find a way to fix what just happened. Footsteps echoing down the hall made me come to a stop.

"Raph," Alon acknowledged me as he approached his study.

Talia walked behind him with her head held high. However, the tight grasp she had on the skirt of her dress betrayed her. My mind and feelings pulled at one another, fighting for dominance. Talia needed to understand how important her role as the lost princess was, yet seeing her so upset at dinner made me want to punch something. Alon gestured for Talia to enter first. She didn't acknowledge me as she passed by.

"You are welcome to join us," Alon said to me. My eyes stayed fixed on Talia's back, looking for a sign whether she wanted me to join or not, but she showed no reaction. I stayed a few feet behind, but followed them in, not entirely sure if it was to support Alon and the cause, or to protect Talia.

"Both of you can take a seat," Alon said, going over to his desk.

"I'd rather stand," Talia said with a small bite in her voice. Her hands stayed firmly clasped behind her back, but she rubbed her thumb against her palm as she peered around the room.

"Suit yourself." Alon sat and steepled his hands in front of his mouth. He directed his attention to Talia. "Would you mind explaining to me what that was about? I thought we had a deal." His eyebrow lifted as he waited for her to answer.

"You couldn't honestly think I would go along with what they were saying," she said, unclasping her hands. "They were talking about a coronation and going on public tours to see the people."

"Yes. Those are all things suitable for a princess."

"But I'm not one!"

I took a step forward, but Alon flicked his gaze to me. I stopped.

"Plus, none of this even matters if you aren't able to find my parents." She crossed her arms. "Any news?" This time Talia lifted her brow.

Alon exhaled and rubbed his forehead. "Do you know what's happening out there right now?" He pointed south. "The King's Guard are searching for you and your parents everywhere. They are going from village to village questioning everyone, and I'm sure they aren't doing it in the most amicable way. My people need to keep their heads down and stay safe. I need you to understand how much bigger this is than you and your parents."

"They are all I care about."

I took a step in front of her. "What about Jemma? And the people of Hattlee? The young women we saved? Or what about your maids at the palace?" I asked. "They are all being affected by this. You know better than anyone how much the people of Landore suffer under Madden's rule." She bit her lip and refused to look at me directly. I thought I might have gotten to her.

"I can't worry about any of that until I find my parents," she said, shrinking into herself.

Alon slammed his fist on his desk, and Talia jumped. "You don't understand what's at stake!"

She reached to her neck. "I do," she whispered. "But I never asked for this. I'm a plain village girl from Gasmere. I'm not a princess or anything else you want me to be," she said.

"Can't you see none of that matters? You are failing to understand the hope that the lost princess symbolizes. The thought of you merely existing threatens Madden's reign more than any army ever could. With you as the lost princess, villagers will question Madden being on the throne and begin to hope for a new future. One that we have been waiting thirty years for."

"But King Madden doesn't believe me to be the real lost princess."

"It doesn't matter. He announced you to the kingdom, and he won't go back on his word. You are the lost princess."

Talia tapped her finger against her collarbone as she narrowed her eyes at Alon. "If you have always believed me to be the lost princess, why did you let me go back to Gasmere after we saved the young women? Why didn't you bring me here right away?"

I leaned forward as Alon remained silent, not allowing any emotion to cross his face.

"And I want the truth," she demanded, crossing her arms.

Alon exhaled. "Because me declaring you as the lost princess wouldn't have meant anything. No one would have believed it. Madden had to be the one to identify and name the lost princess." His eyes softened, and from years of knowing him, I knew he was telling the truth. "I thought it was better to leave you with your family. I assumed Madden would choose a random young woman. I didn't know he would choose you." Alon's weight shifted slightly from one foot to the other. I narrowed my eyes at the movement.

A silent moment passed between them, and I tried to decipher the unsettling feeling I had. Something wasn't adding up. Talia dropped her arms and placed them behind her back, widening her stance.

"Okay," she announced.

"What?" I asked, and Alon leaned forward.

"I will give you five more days to find my parents. In that time, I will go along with being your symbol of hope. I won't contradict whatever people want to believe."

Alon released his breath as he relaxed in his chair. I was still on edge.

"But..." she said. Alon straightened. Her eyes flicked to me for the first time and then went back to Alon. "I want to be trained at The Academy."

"Absolutely not."

I stepped toward Alon. "Sir, it might not be a bad idea." Talia's eyes widened as she looked at me.

"It's too dangerous. Plus, her identity still needs to stay a secret," he said with a tone of authority, but I wasn't willing to back down.

The night she tried to escape, she shared how she felt like a prisoner in Aydencia, just like in the palace. I didn't want that for her. Maybe her being able to train and not being stuck in Skyhall all day would give her some sense of freedom. Plus, with Madden and his guards looking for her, she needed to learn how to protect herself, especially if I wasn't with her. The mere thought of not being able to protect her from him had my blood boiling.

"She can train in private until we announce her to the public. And it might build morale if the Aydencians see their lost princess learning to fight," I argued.

Alon opened his mouth then closed it as he rubbed his chin.

He dipped his head in Talia's direction. "It's a deal. Raph will train you."

I tried to swallow the lump in my throat as I comprehended what training Talia would entail.

She turned to me. "I would like to start tomorrow."

"As you wish." I lowered my chin.

Her eyes danced with excitement, the light in them somewhat returning as she looked at me expectantly. A look that seared itself into my mind. One I would do anything to see again. The moisture in my mouth evaporated. I wouldn't be able to train her and suppress my feelings.

CHAPTER 19

Jules

"WE'RE A FEW MILES out," Luc announced between ragged breaths. He had been scouting ahead.

I relaxed my shoulders. Traveling with over a hundred people was harder than I had anticipated. Especially when the majority were little kids or elderly. My patience was tested at every turn. "Let's keep moving for another mile. Can you find a place for everyone to camp?"

I peered over my shoulder to look at the mass of people, clearly seeing the divide between the callings as they followed with slow, heavy steps. The majority were Hunters, but there was a smattering of Healers, Merchants, and even a few Farmers. I was glad word had somehow gotten to them.

"Of course," Luc said, keeping his eyes on me longer than I liked before jogging ahead. I glanced behind me one more time.

Two mothers walked next to each other. They were talking in hushed tones, but I could see the fear and uncertainty in their eyes. I could see it in all of them. Not only were they tired from traveling and sleeping on the ground for four nights, but there was no guarantee that after all this traveling we would find a safe place for them to stay. We didn't know what would meet us in Hattlee, even if Gil was fairly certain his friends could help us. Plus, knowing that the King's Guard was out there, somewhere, was creating an anxious atmosphere around all of us.

"Drink?" Gil extended a water canteen to me. I guzzled its contents. "Don't worry, there is plenty more where that came from." His lips curved into a smirk, but it didn't reach his eyes. "How are you holding up?" Gil nudged me like he hadn't already asked me that question an hour ago. He had practically glued himself to me for the past three days. And Luc was no better. One of them was always there when I turned around.

"I'm fine." I fought back the urge to massage my temple. I had hardly slept since we left Gasmere, and Gil knew it. We were too exposed traveling with this many people. Regardless, every time I closed my eyes, all I saw was the King's Wraith.

"We will reach Hattlee soon, and it'll all work out," he continued.

I looked away, not wanting him to read me.

"They'll be safe soon. You'll get them there."

Clenching my fists, I shoved down the emotions that were rising in my throat. "You don't know that," I said, making eye contact with him.

"No. But I have faith," he said, lifting his shoulders as he kicked a pebble with his foot.

"In what?" My eyebrows pinched together.

"For starters, you." He bumped my shoulder with his own. I began to roll my eyes. "I'm serious," he said with a laugh. "You're a natural leader. You will ensure these people stay safe. And it's my job to ensure that you stay safe in the process." He couldn't resist winking at the end, which did cause me to roll my eyes. "Life is too short to go around thinking nothing is ever going to work out and that everything will fall apart."

"Hmmm," I said, pressing my lips together, unsure if I agreed. Someone still needed to have a practical outlook on a situation and how it would work out.

"It's like I always say to Raph, you gotta take life by the horns and ride it hard," he said with a mischievous grin.

I covered my mouth to hide my laughter. "You are one of a kind," I said.

"Ahem."

Luc stood in front of us with his arms crossed. He threw a look at Gil before softening his gaze at me. "This will be close enough to Hattlee."

I blew out air and tried my best to ignore the knots in my stomach. "Okay. Gil and I will go in first and talk with the Colans. We will be back in a few hours," I said, gauging the sun.

Luc pressed his lips together but said nothing.

"Keep everyone ready. We will want to move into Hattlee before dark," Gil added, and then gave me a nod.

"We will be back soon," I said to Luc, but I focused my eyes on the group behind me who had also come to a stop. The children were already chasing each other, but the adults stared intently at me. Giving them what I hoped was an encouraging smile, I turned to face Gil. "Let's go."

We said nothing else to each other as we traveled north. However, the silence wasn't uncomfortable, and it didn't take long before we saw the gate into Hattlee.

"Keep your hood up and your head down," Gil said as he pulled his own lower. I followed suit, thankful for the chill in the air that would cause others to have their hoods up so we wouldn't stick out.

I heard the villagers, but I kept my eyes on the ground. We had entered through the main gate of the village, following the road that led into the Penta. The sound of children laughing, parents yelling after their children, and villagers asking for items from the Merchants echoed around me. It made me miss Gasmere. I couldn't help but gaze up to take it in with my eyes.

I stopped. Despite it sounding familiar and the layout being almost identical to Gasmere, there was a mix of colors throughout the crowd of people. I couldn't see a clear distinction between the callings as the villagers were talking and walking around with one another. "How is this possible?" I mumbled.

Gil pulled my cloak, urging me forward again. "Head down," he whispered harshly.

I did what he said, but I couldn't unsee it.

Gil didn't slow his pace until we came to a Healing House. He knocked on the door. And as we waited, I took in my surroundings. The quarter was silent, almost deserted. Very similar to our Artist's quarter. Before I could ask Gil about it, a little girl with long, brown hair opened the door. Her little face lit up the moment Gil pulled back his hood.

"Gil!" she shouted and then jumped into his arms.

He swung her around in circles. "Jemma," he said, squeezing her a little tighter before placing her feet back on the ground.

Her button nose scrunched when her eyes landed on me. "Who's that? Where are the others? Where's Talia?" I frowned when she said Talia's name in a low whisper.

"Unfortunately, none of them could come." Her face dropped with disappointment at Gil's admission. "But this is Jules, Talia's best friend."

Jemma's eyes widened and then narrowed as she inspected me from head to toe. She pulled out a necklace from under her shirt, one I was very familiar with.

I had never been good with kids, but I knelt in front of her. "Tals and I were around your age when I gave that to her. And," I said in a whisper, drawing her attention back up from the pendant, "she told me about the fun she had in Hattlee with you and your family. She said it was the best Harvest Festival she'd ever been to, and it wouldn't have happened without you."

A wide grin covered her face. "What else did she say? Is she going to come back and visit?"

I looked at Gil and stood.

"Jemma, we will answer your questions in a bit, but where are your parents? It's really important we talk with them," Gil said.

"Okay." She grabbed Gil's hand and pulled him through the doorway.

I trailed behind them taking in the familiar scent of different tonics and medicinal herbs. The room was filled with cots arranged in rows with privacy curtains encircling each one. It resembled the Healing House in Gasmere, but there were far more beds than I would ever think necessary. Three of the beds appeared to be occupied, as evidenced by the rumpled sheets, yet no individuals were present.

Jemma led us to the back and through another door. "Mother! Father!" she yelled, stopping us in a hallway.

"What is it, Jemma?" A woman called back.

"Gil and Talia's best friend want to talk to you!"

For a moment, nothing happened, then we heard chairs scraping against the floor and items being moved around. A door to our left flew open. An older man, my guess was Jemma's father, stepped out. A smile took over his face once he took in Gil.

"Gil, it's so good to see you," he said, then gave him a hug with a strong pat on the back. "Did Alon and the others not come with you?"

"No, they had other business to attend to. But they send their regards," Gil said with a beaming smile of his own.

"I'm sorry. Where are my manners?" Jemma's father turned to me. "I'm David Colan." He stuck out his hand, and I returned the gesture.

"Jules," I said. "It's nice to meet you."

"David, don't have them hang out in the hall," the same woman's voice from before said, stepping out of the doorway. Jemma was almost a replica of her with the same sun-kissed brown hair, round face, and small button nose. "We are glad to have you, Jules. I'm Esther," she said, wiping her hand on an apron before extending it to me.

"Yes, any friend of Gil's is a friend of ours," Mr. Colan said with another slap against Gil's back. Gil stumbled forward a little and started choking on his spit.

"We actually," *cough*, "need to talk with you both. It's quite urgent." Gil's tone grew heavier.

Mr. and Mrs. Colan shared a look. "Of course. Come take a seat." Mrs. Colan gestured to the door they had come through, which turned out to be their kitchen. A rectangular table sat near the door while the other side housed the stove with their pots and pans. There were also a variety of herbs being hung to dry.

"Please take a seat," Mr. Colan offered.

I grabbed the chair next to Gil, but Jemma snatched it before I could sit.

"Jules, you can sit here," Mrs. Colan said with a small shake of her head at Jemma.

"What is going on? And how can we help?" Mr. Colan said, cutting right to the chase.

"I'm sure you've heard of what has happened in Gasmere," Gil said, and Mr. and Mrs. Colan nodded solemnly. "Nothing was left standing. The whole village will have to be rebuilt. Plus, the fires injured many villagers when they tried to put them out."

"Those poor families." Mrs. Colan clutched at her heart.

Gil continued, "With winter already here, the ground has started to freeze, so no permanent buildings can be constructed until it thaws."

"Many families are without a place to sleep and the village is running out of supplies," I cut in, letting the desperation I felt seep into my words. "All our crops and storage houses were destroyed as well."

"And you are wondering if we would house some of these families?" Mr. Colan asked with a strange smile on his face.

"Yes," Gil and I said at the same time.

"Anthony is going to brag about this for weeks," he said, shaking his head. "We have been planning for this. We have about sixty cots available here."

My lips parted. I truly couldn't believe what I was hearing.

"How did you—I mean—wow, thank you," Gil said, looking at me with a hopeful smile.

"We had a feeling families might come through, and then our latest three guests being from Gasmere sort of confirmed it," Mr. Colan explained.

Jemma had been surprisingly quiet the whole time but perked up at the mention of their guests. "You just missed them! They left this morning." Her lips turned down before twisting into a mischievous grin. "But they were a lot of fun to bother. Especially the big one with the scar. He was my favorite." She giggled.

Gil and I looked at each other with the same worried expression.

"What were the names of the visitors?" Gil asked.

"Julian, Oliver, and the one Jemma is referring to is Kasper. Do you know them?" Mrs. Colan asked.

I grabbed the edge of the table. He was here. He could still be here.

"My dear, what is wrong?" Mrs. Colan placed her hand on top of mine. "You are as white as a sheet."

"When did you say they left?" Gil's voice was quiet, like he was afraid of the answer.

"Umm, probably an hour or two ago." Mr. Colan looked at his wife with a frown.

"We have to go!" I pushed my chair back. "What if he found them?" I said to Gil.

"What's going on? What if who found who?" Everyone stood.

"I'm sorry, David, we don't have time to explain," Gil said, heading to the door. "We will be back."

I followed Gil out the door and through the rows of cots, hitting many of the beds along the way as I tried to match his speed. At the door, I nearly ran into Gil as he spun around to face the Colans. They stood in the middle of the room with shocked expressions.

"Whatever you do, never let those men come back through this door," Gil practically hissed before he threw it open and exited.

We broke out into a sprint, not bothering to keep our heads down or make sure our hoods stayed up. Gil kept pace with me, but I could tell he was holding back.

We made it to the Penta, and he took the lead. Our pace slowed a fraction as we dodged between people. A man carrying an armful of supplies cut right between Gil and me. There was no time for me to change direction. My shoulder collided with him, and we stumbled to the ground. Packages littered the area around us.

"I'm sorry," I said breathlessly, pushing back onto my feet.

"No harm done," the young man said as he locked eyes with me.

My heart stopped.

I scanned over his tight brown tunic and then back up to his familiar face. He was with the kidnappers. He was a part of the King's Guard.

"Jules," Gil called from behind me.

The guard flicked his eyes to Gil and then back to me before he opened his mouth. "Your High—Kasper!" he shouted over his shoulder.

I sprinted toward Gil, frantically motioning him to keep running. I could hear a commotion behind me, but I didn't dare turn around. Only one thought kept racing through my mind.

He's here.

CHAPTER 20

Kasper

"Your High—Kasper!" Julian shouted from behind me. The supplies we had purchased were scattered at his feet, and he stood wide-eyed, pointing in front of him. "It's them!"

I narrowed my eyes, trying to glimpse the two figures darting through the crowd of people. Unfortunately, their faces remained a blur, but one detail stood out—vibrant blond hair. Julian's expression confirmed my suspicions. They were rebels.

I left the stall I had been waiting in line at. I ran past Julian and shouted, "Get Oliver!"

The rebels were leaving the Penta and heading toward the village gates. I pressed my legs harder. The closest one to me was most likely a woman with long brown hair. Adrenaline coursed through me at the idea of being able to catch a new lead.

From the gates, they headed south, opting to stay off the road and head into the trees. Once I reached the tree line, I lost them, but I continued south until I was further away from the village. I held my breath, listening to my surroundings. An actual grin pulled at my lips as the sound of pounding feet and twigs breaking filled my ears.

They had changed course and were headed west. These two could be my last chance. I couldn't afford to lose them. The thought of what my father would do if I failed pushed me to dig deeper. Footprints in the light dusting of snow on the ground caught my eye, and my heart pounded against my chest as I followed the trail.

Finally, I caught sight of the woman. She was slower than the other one. I veered to the left to keep her in my line of sight. A burning sensation surged through my legs, but it fueled my determination. I pushed harder, gaining ground on her. There was a quiver and bow strapped to her back, and I felt a wave of gratitude at not having my sword weighing me down. The whip concealed around my waist would be sufficient. Her green cloak trailed behind her.

I could almost grab it.

With one final push into the ground, I leaped and tackled her. A groan ripped through her as we hit the hard ground. But she didn't waste any time. Her head collided with my chin, and I lost my grip on her. She was rolling away to stand.

The woman fitted an arrow, and I was ready to anticipate her next move.

I dodged to the left when she released it. Her hair obscured most of her face, making it difficult for me to get a clear view of her. She took her aim with a second arrow, and I grabbed my whip, prepared to defend myself.

With a quick flick of my whip, I deflected the arrow. It fell to the ground broken. Her body stiffened, but she didn't stop. She reached for another, her movements fluid and precise. A third arrow headed my way. I managed to evade it too, but barely. She was skilled.

Her partner was approaching us. I needed to handle her quickly. When she reached for another arrow, I seized the opportunity. With a swift motion, I snapped my whip. The crack echoed through the air as it connected with her arm. She let out a scream as the whip wrapped tightly around it. I pulled her toward me, and her bow fell.

Desperate, she reached for her hip, presumably for a dagger. Her hand fumbled when trying to unsheathe it. I pulled the whip from her arm. With a crack, I dislodged the dagger she had freed. She let out another cry as she cradled her hand.

An arrow whizzed by my ear. A hot sensation filled its place. Her partner, a blond man, was closing in on me. The fire behind his eyes told me he was ready for a fight. I shifted my focus to him, knowing she couldn't do much at this point. However, she jumped to her feet and took a fighting stance in front of me, allowing me take in her familiar face.

My eyes widened with recognition while hers narrowed, burning with hostility. Her fists tightened, and I noticed the trail of blood running down one of them. Silence hung heavy in the air as I tried to piece everything together.

Searing pain shot through my thigh and a low, guttural groan escaped my lips. I looked to find an arrow jutting out from my leg. Looking up, my heart pounded in my chest as a fist swiftly connected with my face with a sickening thud. The impact made my vision blur momentarily.

I clutched my throbbing nose and wetness seeped between my fingers. Taking a shaky step back, my leg faltered from the pain of the arrow lodged in my thigh. My grip tightened around the leather handle of my whip, the rough texture digging into my palm. I readied myself to retaliate, prepared to lash my whip across her face. However, before I could release it, she moved away from me.

They were running away. I roared and cracked my whip into the air, knowing I couldn't catch them in this condition.

I couldn't believe it was her. The same woman we had kidnapped. And she had gotten away from me again, but this time she took my last bit of restraint with her.

CHAPTER 21

Talia

As I stepped through the trees, a sense of relief washed over me. There wasn't a single soul in sight, not even Raph, and I needed a moment alone to prepare myself for what was about to happen. Yes, I wanted to be trained, but when Alon had ordered Raph to be the one to do it, my whole body seized up. The mere thought of me and him being alone together was making my heart rate quicken.

The training ground stretched before me. Directly in the middle, there was a large ring carved into the ground where Raph had sparred with that young student. I swallowed, hoping Raph wouldn't make me fight against him on day one. The dozen elevated platforms past the ring caught my attention, having no idea what they could be used for. But then I spotted something familiar, a row of meticulously arranged targets for archery. At least I wasn't starting out with no skills. I unclasped my cloak, pulling it off my shoulders as I felt the heat from the noon sun. It was the only time we could train because the students would be eating, allowing us to be undisturbed. As I turned to the right, my eyes met a colossal wooden wall, behind which lay a collection of strange and foreboding contraptions.

I rolled my shoulders back, attempting to release the fear climbing up my spine. Backing out of this was not an option. If I had to search for my parents while the King's Guard was looking for me, I needed to be capable of protecting myself. Plus, with all the talk about a war, it seemed likely that I would have to ensure the safety of my parents and myself until it all blew over and we could find somewhere safe to live.

Voices drew my attention behind me toward the academy. Raph, Adira, and Hafsa were walking out of the doors. Raph and Adira were in some sort of serious conversation until they spotted me leaning against one of the platforms. Adira smiled, but Raph kept his face tight as they approached.

"Adira and Hafsa will be in charge of your training," Raph said in a clipped voice.

"But Alon said—"

"The deal was for you to be trained, I don't have to be the one to do it."

A sharp pain hit me in the chest as a sense of disappointment washed over me. "And what will you be doing?" I asked

"Supervising." He moved to a different platform, and leaned against one of the poles with his arms crossed. I bit my tongue and told myself it was better this way.

"We should get started," Adira said, not fully able to hide the awkwardness in her voice.

Hafsa placed two waterskins on the platform. "I think this was a brilliant idea." Hafsa's eyes shone with excitement. "Everyone should know how to defend themselves, especially a princess."

Knots formed in my stomach. They didn't know the real reason why I was demanding to be trained, and I wasn't going to share.

"Ready, Princess?" Adira asked with a raised brow.

"Yes." I rubbed the back of my neck as I followed her and Hafsa into the middle of the field.

I didn't know what to expect in terms of learning how to fight. But I never would have guessed it would begin with a ridiculous amount of running. My lungs were on fire as I desperately tried to inhale more air. Adira had me run around the entire training grounds three times. By the halfway point of the first lap, my legs felt heavy as lead. Nevertheless, I refused to feel powerless and unable to protect those I love. I persevered through the pain and completed the three laps—barely.

"Good," Adira yelled from a platform. "Now we will do some exercises that will warm up your body."

I snorted. I couldn't get any warmer.

Hafsa met me in the middle of the circle and led me through different poses and stretches. At first, I was relieved that it was going to be a lot easier than running, but that quickly changed.

"Are these poses a part of Reeyu?" I asked in a shaky voice, remembering the name Gil used to describe the form of fighting Hafsa and Nadav used.

"Yes, they are the fundamentals. It is what we learn first," she said, giving me a side-glance. She was holding the same pose as me, but her muscles weren't shaking uncontrollably. "One must be able to control their body in the small movements before attempting to control it in a fight. And don't worry, shaking is good. It means your muscles are working," she said in a calm voice.

"I don't think I can hold it much longer," I stuttered before I collapsed onto the ground.

"I think that's enough." Hafsa reached her hand out to help me stand.

"Everything alright?" Adira asked, jogging over to us.

"Yeah," I said, shaking my arms out. "What's next?"

"Defensive training," Adira declared, and I dropped my shoulders slightly.

My disappointment didn't go unnoticed.

"Knowing how to defend and protect yourself is crucial. Everything you just did to strengthen your body will help with that," Hafsa explained. "You have awakened your muscles to be on guard and more alert."

"Your reaction time to an attack is critical," Adira chimed in.

"That makes sense," I said, still a little miffed. My treacherous eyes drifted to where Raph stood, wondering if he would have taught me offensive moves right away. He hadn't moved or said anything this whole time. He just glared.

"Here." Adira tossed me a waterskin. I took a long drink before pouring some of it on my flushed face.

"The first thing to remember, if someone attacks you, is to stay calm." Adira grabbed the water from me and handed it to Hafsa. "The moment you panic, your mind won't be able to focus. Hafsa and I are going to show you some different moves you can use based on how someone may attack you."

Adira gave a nod to Hafsa. Hafsa instantly sprung on her and grabbed Adira from behind. She placed a hand over her mouth and the other around her midsection.

"Being a princess, many will assume you are weak and have no fighting skills. This will most likely be how they will attack. One hand over your mouth to silence you and the other around your midsection to carry you away," Hafsa explained.

"So, what do I do?" I felt anxious at the mere idea of being in this kind of situation.

Adira slammed her foot on the ground right next to Hafsa's and then threw her head back as if to headbutt Hafsa in the face. Even though Adira didn't touch her, Hafsa reacted as if she had.

"You go for one of their lower extremities, which will cause them to buckle forward, and then ram your head into theirs. They will release their grip, and that is when you run." Adira's face went serious. "Do not stay and try to fight them or look to see who it is. The moment their hands are off of you, run. Do you understand?"

"Yes," I answered, but still unsure if I could go through with it when the time came. The first time I intentionally hurt someone was when I punched Jacob in the face. I wasn't prone to violence, but my drive to survive and protect others was winning out.

They demonstrated a handful of other maneuvers and had me try to get out of them. The sun began its descent and not only was my body fried, but so was my brain at this point.

"Ugh!" I released the tension in my body as Hafsa's arm wrapped around me again. I hadn't been successful at evading any of her attacks. She released her grip. "I'm too slow," I said, pressing my hands against the sides of my head and releasing them.

Footsteps pulled our attention. Raph stalked toward us, but his eyes bore into me. I stood my ground, fighting the urge to take a step back when he stopped mere inches from me.

My chest raised and fell rapidly as my lungs fought for more air. He stared down at me, his eyes full of some intense emotion.

"You need to widen your stance," he said, tapping his foot against one of mine.

I blinked a few times, getting my mind and body back in sync. I followed his orders and gave a side-glance to Adira, but she had already taken a step back with a smug look on her face. Apparently, she had no problem with him taking over. I jerked my head back to Raph as he rested his palm on my stomach. Heat flared to my reddened cheeks.

"This is where your movements come from." His hand pressed against my stomach and for a second my breath left my lungs. "Pretend there's a ball in your center. Compress it."

I closed my eyes, trying to visualize what he meant and ignore the warmth from his hand.

"Open your eyes," he said, removing his hand.

Raph attacked the moment my eyes opened. I stepped back with one foot, compressing the fake ball in my stomach, and swiveled my body to the side. Raph's outstretched hands grasped for air.

"That's it," Hafsa said with a clap.

I let myself smile.

"It's a start," Raph said, crossing his arms.

My smile dropped. I opened my mouth to ask him what his problem was, but he spoke first.

"You're done for the day," he said, then pivoted toward Adira. "We need to talk."

Adira didn't respond, but she kept her smirk.

"Hafsa, will you please escort Her Highness back to Skyhall?" he asked, but it came out as more of a command.

"Of course," she answered, but looked at me.

I was too tired to fight him. I was already wondering how I would make it up the mountain. Hafsa and I left the training grounds, but as we reached the tree line, Raph's voice filled the air.

"I know what you're doing, so stop."

I looked at Hafsa, but she kept her eyes forward. The marking on her chin pulled tight as she smashed her lips together. It reminded me of the countless questions I had about her and Nadav and the King- dom of Nefali.

"You and Nadav are from Nefali, right?" I asked as we walked through the trees.

"Yes," she said.

"Can I ask you a question?" She gave me a closed smile while bobbing her head. "Why are you here?" I asked, feeling slightly embarrassed for even asking the question.

She released a long exhale. "Our kingdoms used to be great allies, sharing in each other's wealth and resources. However, when Madden took the throne, he shut off all ties with us. Our kingdom has also been awaiting your return."

My steps faltered as we approached the first set of stairs. "What does that have to do with you and Nadav?"

"A couple of years ago our king and queen sent a few of our people on a scouting trip to see what was happening in your kingdom." I winced when she said *my* kingdom. "It was complete luck they crossed paths with Alon during his yearly trip into Llycia. He informed them about Aydencia and how they were building their own army. When they returned to Nefali and relayed everything, our king and queen ordered Nadav and me to help assist in the removal of Madden in any way possible," Hafsa finished.

"But what could you two do?" I asked, mostly to myself, not realizing how it sounded. "I...I mean...I know you are incredible fighters, but it's just the two of you."

"Your question is fair, Your Highness," she said with a dip of her head. Her smile was genuine, but it didn't lessen the heat in my cheeks. "But never underestimate the difference one person can make." She finished with a raise of her eyebrow. "May I ask you a question?"

"Sure," I said, noticing that we took a longer route to Skyhall.

"Why do you resist the idea that you are the lost princess?"

"Besides the obvious lack of freedom?" I raised my eyebrows. "Seriously, I don't understand why anyone would want to be of noble birth."

Hafsa's pace slowed and the pained look on her face made me question whether I had said something to offend her.

My mouth dried. "Because...because other than my looks, there is no evidence that I am." I let her walk in front of me. "And nothing good will come of it," I said under my breath.

She stayed silent as we ascended the last part of the mountain to reach Skyhall. We walked the rest of the way to the room I was staying in without sharing another word. I opened the door and walked inside, giving her an awkward side-smile.

"Good job today, and thank you for being honest," she said with a small bow of her head.

I closed the door slowly. I shouldn't have said what I did, but it was how I felt. Nothing good had come from me being the lost princess, and it would only get worse for those that I loved. I grabbed my chest as the memory of Catherine being whipped entered my mind.

No. I wanted nothing to do with being the lost princess. All I wanted was to find my parents.

I was about to take a bath, but the mere thought of my parents made me turn back around. Instead, I left the room and headed for Alon's study. I hadn't seen him yet, so I wanted to ask if he had received any news.

I made my way down the hall that went deeper into the mountain, feeling the temperature drop with every step I took. It was dark and eerily quiet, and I was about to turn around. However, as I approached Alon's door, I saw light coming from underneath. I raised my arm to knock, but voices inside made me pause.

I pressed my ear to the door and heard Alon's voice. My ears rang and the next thing I knew, I was running.

CHAPTER 22

Raph

"Enter," Alon called from the other side of the door. I dropped my hand and entered. "How'd training go?" he asked, not looking up from his desk.

I stood with my arms behind my back. "You were right. It's a mistake. All that will come of it is her getting hurt. She has no idea how to fight."

He wrote something. "I'm sure you've had students who started out in the same place. I have faith in you."

"Alon." My voice was tense and he lifted his gaze.

He set his pen down and arched an eyebrow. "Why the sudden change of heart?"

I couldn't tell him the real reason. That Adira refusing to train her unless I was present was torture for me. That I needed to distance myself from the princess, because every time I was near her I lost all reason and control. I couldn't admit my weakness. "She will end up hurt. It's a bad idea," I answered.

"It's making her cooperate with our plans, and it will help spark a fire in everyone once we announce her like you said. I don't see how it's a bad idea." He reached to lift his pen again. "Unless you have a different reason as to why it's a bad idea?" he asked, arching an eyebrow.

"No. I...I just—"

"She'll be fine. Just make sure she doesn't get too injured. I didn't hand you my old position for no reason." He dropped his head, a sign there was nothing further to discuss.

I tightened my grip around my wrist. The same unease I had felt before when he talked with Talia washed over me. He was hiding something. I had always trusted him without question, but bringing Talia to Aydencia had somehow changed things. "Have you set a date for when you will announce her?"

"Soon." His voice was low.

"According to our agreement, we have four more days. Unless you have already received information about her parents?" I asked, then clenched my jaw, frustrated that he wouldn't tell me what was going on, especially with innocent lives on the line.

Alon exhaled, then banged the pen on the table. "It's handled."

"I won't send my students to their death." My frustration matched his.

"Watch it." His words were an order. "I've been planning this for eighteen years, and every student who enters The Academy knows what they are signing up for. They have decided to fight for a better future. If there was another way, we would have taken it."

"Why can't we assassinate him? Then we wouldn't have to bother with a war or a lost princess at all."

He rubbed his temple. "The people of Landore might not love him, but they fear him and his power. He has an heir that could take his place, and I doubt the prince is any better than his father." The fire inside me grew hotter at the thought of Prince Kasper on the throne. "Madden has many who are loyal to him. Especially those he brought up with him. Who is to say that if we killed him and put Talia on the throne that one of them wouldn't kill her?" He paused, and I realized my breathing had quickened.

"Raph, it's about power. People fall in line with those who they think have the most power, and those who can take care of them. We need to show our strength to the people of Landore and that we can provide a better life for them. Under Queen Talia, we will have the support of another kingdom again, and Landore will thrive."

"What if she says no?" I asked.

Alon allowed his face to drop, showing how tired he really was. "She won't."

"What do you mean?" Fear replaced the anger.

"It doesn't matter," he answered, hardening again.

The anger clawed its way up my throat, and before I knew it, I was approaching Alon's desk. "What do you have planned for her?" I slammed my hands down.

"Control yourself!" He stood from his chair. "I did not spend the last year working tirelessly to spread that rumor about a lost princess for some stubborn eighteen-year-old girl to bring everything we have fought for down in flames."

I took a couple steps back. "You...you started that rumor?"

"Yes." Regret filled his eyes.

"But those young women who were kidnapped..."

"An unfortunate price to be paid."

"But..." I shook my head, unable to finish.

"We had to see if Madden would take the bait. And he did much more than that." I couldn't believe what I was hearing. "We needed Madden to believe an heir survived. We needed the people of Landore to question his legitimacy."

I opened my mouth, but Alon's door opened.

"Adira," Alon said, sternly. "I hope you have a good reason for barging in."

She leaned against the doorframe, fiddling with one of her throwing knives. "I thought you should know I saw Princess Talia running out the front door." She flipped the knife in the air and caught it. "And she was coming from this direction."

Alon and I turned to each other.

"Find her," he ordered.

I marched out of the room, but not before turning to Adira. "Are you going to help?"

"I think you'd better handle this one," she said, tapping the blade on my shoulder. "She can't truly leave anyways." She shrugged.

I pushed past her and headed straight to the front door. The frustration over this whole situation continued to rise inside of me.

Releasing a groan, I tightened my grip around the railing of the bridge. The cool stone against my skin did nothing to calm me. It had been an hour, and I had no clue where she could have run off to. I searched the docks, thinking she might try her hand at stealing a boat again, but there was no sign of her. I checked the open trade shops and even the academy.

I pushed forward and scanned the area below me. The sun had already set, which meant most of the people had retreated to their homes. This should've made it easier to spot her, but she remained hidden.

Where would she go? What would make her feel safe?

I whipped my head to the right, chastising myself for not thinking of it sooner, and I took off for the trees. There weren't many areas on this side of the mountain with trees. Only a cluster surrounding the academy, which I had already checked, so there was one option left.

I followed the overgrown stone path that led deeper into the trees. I hadn't been there since returning, but the thick and lush foliage along with the trees wrapped in vines and moss felt familiar.

After a while, the sound of rushing water filled the air, alerting me I was close. The path opened to a clearing where the Remembrance Tree stood. The tree's trunk filled most of the space, wider than four of me standing side by side, and its high branches reached into the night sky. I remained still, scanning the area. My heart dropped into my stomach at no sign of her, but then I noticed a slight movement coming from behind the tree.

Talia sat against it. Her knees were pulled into her chest as she faced the large waterfall, unaware of my presence. I stepped over the ring of smooth stones encircling the tree base. Quietly, I maneuvered around the tree until I stood directly behind her. Placing my hand on the rough bark, I took a deep breath and gathered my thoughts.

"You shouldn't be out here alone," I said.

She didn't move, and for a moment I thought she didn't hear me, but she said, "I'm not staying. Tell Alon the deal's off." She kept her gaze trained ahead.

I moved in front of her. "The deal isn't off," I said, but the last part came out as a whisper as she looked at me with tear-stained cheeks.

Her eyes narrowed. "If you believe I'm going to stay here after learning that everything started because of *him*," she spat, pointing with her finger, "then you're an idiot." She choked out as more tears fell.

"What are you talking about?"

"I heard everything! How Alon started the rumors. And how he was the reason Jules and the others were kidnapped. He is the reason King Madden was looking for the lost princess, and why my parents are missing and I'm here, alone." Her hand shook as she wiped the tears away.

"Those things aren't Alon's fault. They're Madden's. He is the enemy," I stated, not truly convinced I believed my words but knowing my orders would be to get her to.

"Of course you are going to side with him." She dropped her gaze back to the water.

"He only started the rumors to set the people of Landore against Madden. He didn't intend for any of the other stuff to happen." A part of me couldn't believe I was defending him. The sting of betrayal was still embedded into my heart.

"Are you sure?" she asked, looking up. "Because from where I'm sitting, it sure looks like he was playing me from the moment we met."

I didn't have an answer. The truth was, I didn't know what to believe any more. I had so many questions for Alon. It was difficult to process the fact that he had been keeping me in the dark about all of this. Despite my efforts to remain loyal to him and the cause, anger and hurt swelled within me.

I sat next to her. She tensed, but she didn't move away. I leaned against the tree and stared at the descending water. "I don't know," I said, raking my fingers through my hair. "I found out tonight, like you. And before Alon could explain, Adira told us you ran away."

She peered at me.

"I'm not blaming you for running away. I get it," I said, shaking my head. "I wanted to leave the moment he said he started the rumors, but I also needed answers." I focused on her, needing her to really hear me. "I have known Alon for seven years, and the man I know would have a good reason for doing what he did. Isn't it worth staying to find out the truth?" I asked, needing the truth to fix the conflicting emotions inside of me.

She stared at me, her ice-blue eyes piercing the inside of me. "I'll hear him out. But I don't trust him."

"I wouldn't expect you to," I said, feeling the pressure lift from my shoulders, but at the same time a heavy rock settled in my stomach.

We let the roar of the waterfall fill the air.

"What is this place?" she asked, looking up at the tree and then back at the waterfall.

"It's a special place for those who live here," I said, following the water as it hit the pool below, causing it to glow purple. The whole river glowed purple at night. "Some say it's even sacred. They found it shortly after discovering Aydencia and saw the tree as a beacon of hope. It reminded them that no matter what had happened, they would endure." I leaned my head back against the tree. "They call it the Remembrance Tree, to not only remember the loved ones that they lost but to remember how grateful they were to have found this place."

"And the stones?" she asked, sitting forward and looking at them more intently.

"They're a personal memorial for the lives lost and also the ones that have been gained." I observed as her eyes scanned over each one in front of us.

"It's beautiful," she said.

"Yes," I answered, noticing how the reflection of the moon from the water lit up her face.

She leaned against the tree and wrapped her arms around herself, rubbing her hands up and down. She didn't have a cloak or anything besides her tunic.

I removed my overcoat. "Here." She leaned in so I could place it over her shoulders.

"Thank you." Her voice was soft as I lowered my arms. "What happened?" she asked.

I followed her gaze to my rolled-up sleeve, which revealed the burn on my arm. I reached to cover it, but she stopped me. My breath escaped as I gazed into her caring eyes. She looked up at me through her lashes.

"It was the second time I failed at saving someone." Releasing my breath, I removed my arm from her touch and looked out upon the flowing water. I only let certain memories come to the forefront of my mind and this particular one I kept buried deep. "It was shortly after my mother passed. I was on the streets of Llycia, alone. I wasn't the only orphan living on the streets. There were a few of us, but we kept to ourselves. I was in a pretty bad spot. I hadn't eaten for days, and I was about to give up until a girl a few years younger than me found me in an alley and gave me some stale bread. She stayed with me from that day on and together we learned to survive. Until—" I dropped my gaze to the burn. "I failed her."

Talia reached out to me, but she let her hand drop back in her lap.

"It was a cold winter night, and she had missed our meeting time. But I knew where she would be. She was fascinated with the ocean and spent most of her time by the docks. By the time I got there, the sun had vanished, and the docks were fairly deserted, which allowed me to hear it.

"Her faint cries were carried by the wind. I ran as fast as I could, but when I found her, she wasn't alone. A man was placing her unconscious body in the back of a wagon." I felt as if the scene played out in front of me all over again. "There was a lit torch on the back of the wagon, and as I tried to fight the man off and reach for her, I got burned. The next thing I remember is waking on the cold, dark streets alone and she was gone."

"Raph..." My name left her lips in a whisper, stirring something in me I didn't understand. I turned to her. Her gaze was unrelenting, trying to see straight into my soul. And for once I didn't close her out, I allowed her to see the brokenness inside of me.

She gently placed her hand against my cheek. Heat ignited throughout my whole body and all I wanted to do was lean into her touch. For her to lift the weight that had been tied around my heart for years. She opened her mouth, then closed it again, but it drew my eyes to her full, soft lips. When I looked back up, I knew the brokenness in my eyes had shifted to something else, something like desire, because I saw it reflected in her eyes.

The space between us diminished. I could feel the gentle brush of her breath against my face, a warmth that sent a shiver down my spine. I stole a fleeting glance at her lips, needing to experience their softness against mine. But like in the clearing, I knew I couldn't kiss her. She was hurting, and most importantly, she was the lost princess.

I leaned back and slowly brushed her hair away from her face, allowing my fingertips to graze her smooth skin before dropping my hand. Pain flashed across her eyes before she turned to face the water. I wanted to say something, to try and explain, but no words came out. Instead, I remained by her side. She lowered her head on my shoulder. I allowed myself to be comforted by her closeness and to give into my desires and ignore the part of me that knew Alon would disapprove.

"Promise me one thing, Raph," she said. "If you hear any news of my parents, you'll tell me."

"I promise," I said and meant it.

CHAPTER 23

Jules

"Where have you been?" Luc asked, approaching us as we entered the makeshift camp. "What happened?" His eyes widened as he took in my bandaged hand and Gil's ripped tunic.

"We ran into some trouble," Gil whispered as he focused on the small crowd growing behind Luc.

"We need to move out, and we are going to have to split up," I said, fixing the blood-soaked bandage.

A look of confusion crossed Luc's face. "The sun is setting. It will be dark within the hour."

I stepped closer to him. "We ran into the King's Wraith." His jaw dropped. "He knows we are in the area and will be searching for us. We can't stay," I said, peering over his shoulder at the hundred-plus people we had with us. Fear for their lives wrapped tightly around my throat.

Luc gave me a curt nod.

"You'll take sixty of them into the vil—"

"No. I'm staying with you," Luc said, giving a side-eye to Gil, who in turn took a step closer to me.

I kept my gaze on Luc. "We need someone to escort these people to Hattlee."

"Why can't he escort them?" Luc asked.

I blew out the air in my lungs, not wanting to explain how Gil couldn't leave me because he had made a promise to Tals. Grabbing Luc's wrist, I pulled him off to the side. I gave Gil a look over my shoulder with a slight shake of my head as he stepped toward Luc and me.

"We don't have time for this," I said, coming to a stop. "You will take sixty of them to Hattlee."

"I'm not going to leave you with him." Luc crossed his arms. "Your father would agree with me."

"My father is the one who placed me in charge, and this is my decision."

"Do you care for him?"

"What?" I choked on my own spit as heat flared to my cheeks.

"Do you *care* for him?"

"Yes. I mean, no. I..." My words died off as I didn't know how to answer him.

"What about me?" Luc's lips pressed into a firm line. I didn't want to hurt him, but I also couldn't lie to him. I'd never had feelings for him and I never would.

"I... I—"

"Don't." He lifted his palm. "I don't need to hear you say it. I'll take the sixty to Hattlee." He lowered his head.

"We left a trail leading west, so you should be safe," I said, trying to ease the awkwardness. "Enter through the Healer's quarter and go straight to the Healing House. The Colans will expect you. Say you're friends of Gil's and mine."

"What about you two?" Luc said, not able to hide the distaste of putting Gil and me in the same sentence.

"We will take the remaining people and head out for another village tonight. We will meet you back in Gasmere when we have found a place for everyone," I answered.

"Okay." His voice was tense.

I reached my hand out to touch his forearm. "Luc, it wasn't ever going to—"

He pulled his arm away. "I'll see you in Gasmere, Jules." He turned away and walked toward a group of people.

I looked out at the people as I made my way back to Gil. Most of the kids had settled down, on their mothers' laps, asleep. The adults were staring in my direction, their faces tired and scared. I took a deep breath, wishing my father was here to help motivate them. I didn't have his charisma.

"You got this." Gil placed his hand on my shoulder.

Stepping around Gil, I approached the group of expectant faces and relayed the new plan. Fortunately, there were enough people who stepped forward to be part of the group that would make the trip to the village near Hattlee. Gil and I wasted no time guiding our group toward the village before the sun had completely set.

"This is far enough," Gil said for the third time.

"A little further," I answered through my teeth. We had been walking for hours in the night, trying to approach the village from the north, but I couldn't calm the fear inside of me.

"Jules, they need rest. They can't go any further."

"Yes, they can."

He grabbed my wrist, and I ripped my hand away. "Look at them," he said.

"I know, but their lives are at stake. The King's Wraith could be right behind us!"

"Tell them to set up camp for the night," Gil said over his shoulder to one of the older boys.

"No," I said, turning around. "We are—"

Gil grabbed my wrist again and led me a good distance away from everyone. "Look. At. Them." He released his hold.

My throat felt as if it was on fire as I held back my emotions. "I can't." A tear trailed down my cheek. "I can't. Gil, I can't fail them."

"You won't." His brow furrowed. "What is really going on?" he asked, reaching for me, but I stepped back. I couldn't accept his comfort. If I did, I would crumble. Biting my lip, I shook my head. "You can trust me."

"You wouldn't understand."

"Try me," he challenged.

Lifting my head to the stars, I released my breath, watching the white cloud of air disappear. "My whole life has been planned out for me since the day I was born. I was always going to become a Hunter, follow in my parents' footsteps, and one day become the next leader of Gasmere." I wrapped my arms around me. "And I took comfort in that. It was who I was, and everyone knew it. But *now* my future is uncertain," I said, throwing my hands in the air. "And I blame Talia for some of it, which makes me feel even worse." The tears fell faster, but Gil remained still, hardly showing any reaction. "Ever since I was kidnapped, I haven't been able to shake this feeling of fear and that no matter what decision I make it will fail. I'm just...I'm just so scared," I finished, feeling some pressure from my chest release, but also feeling extremely exposed.

"I get it," he said, taking a small step closer. "Everything you're feeling is understandable. Being scared and having to deal with fear is something everyone deals with. You aren't alone."

"Right," I said, flicking my eyes upward.

"I'm serious. Why do you think I'm constantly making jokes? It's my way of dealing with fear. And that's what you have to do. You can recognize the fear, but don't let it control you. You control it." His gaze locked solely on me. "There is so much strength inside you."

My whole body felt warm, and I couldn't tell if it was because of my crying or Gil's words. However, as he kept looking at me, my heart raced.

"Thank you," I said in a whisper.

He reached out and wrapped his strong hand around mine. He gave it a gentle squeeze before he dropped his hand with a shrug. "I can be known to drop a few lines of wisdom here and there."

"Right," I said with a small laugh. "We should probably head back."

"After you." He gave a bow, extending one arm out in front of him.

I walked past him, wondering if what he told me about making jokes was true.

"How are we going to find the Elders?" Gil asked in a harsh whisper as we walked through the village's Penta.

Voices of the villagers filled the air as we kept our hoods up and heads down. The busy morning atmosphere caught me by surprise because we expected a smaller crowd. Thankfully, we had yet to spot any of the King's Guard, but we were definitely drawing attention.

Two men stood next to each other and stared at us with obvious distaste. One of them whispered something to the other one, which caused the first man to walk away. "I don't think that will be a problem," I answered as I continued to lead Gil toward the village's Meeting House.

As we approached the stairs to the entrance of the Meeting House, the doors flew open and a man wearing gray walked out with his arm in a sling. Behind him was the same man who had left his friend. The man with the sling locked eyes with us and hurried down the stairs.

"Who are you? And what do you want?" he asked in one breath.

I lifted my chin so he could see my face. "We are seeking an audience with the Elders of this village."

"I'm an Elder for the Merchants—state your business." His eyes kept flicking behind us as if he was expecting someone else to show up. That's when I noticed that one of his eyes had a yellowish bruise underneath it.

"I think it would be best if we could discuss it in private."

He released his breath. "Okay. But make it quick." He turned to the man behind him and thanked him, then he walked back up the stairs. I grabbed Gil's arm and followed.

The layout of the Meeting House was very similar to Gasmere's except for the people that were currently occupying ours. The Elder didn't stop his quick pace until he ushered us into a room and closed the door behind us.

Once inside, we pulled our hoods back.

The man released a gasp when he saw Gil. I shook my head, berating Gil in my mind. I had told him to stay behind because his hair would make things worse, but he refused to let me go without him.

"We don't mean any harm," Gil said, raising his hands.

"Are you with them? The re...rebels?" The Elder stammered out.

"No," I said. "We are from Gasmere. The King's Guard burned down our village."

The Elder opened his mouth and then looked at his arm.

"And I'm guessing they have already paid your village a visit?" Gil asked.

"Yes. They separated the callings and interviewed nearly every villager. A guard named Sal wasn't too polite to us Elders." I clenched my hands. "But they left us with a warning that if we were to see any strangers, we were to notify the guards stationed here instantly." His gaze flicked to the door, fear clear in his eyes.

"We understand," Gil said.

"We are seeking refuge for some of our women, children, and elderly," I said, stepping forward. "Just until the ground thaws. We have about fifty that need shelter. We left sixty in Hattlee, but they couldn't take any more than that."

"I'm sorry. We can't—"

"Please! They have been traveling for days and need to rest. Will you at least ask the other Elders?"

He shifted his weight from one foot to the other. "Wait here. Don't leave this room," he said before walking out the door.

"Do you think they will take them in?" I asked Gil the moment the door closed.

He pressed his lips together. "I don't know. He was pretty freaked out."

"I know." I paced the room as Gil leaned against the wall.

It felt like hours before the door opened again. The same Elder squeezed through and then closed it right away.

"We will take thirty. No more," he announced.

I brought my hand to my heart relieved. "Thank you."

"We can't promise their safety if the King's Guard takes action against them."

"We wouldn't expect you to," Gil said.

"They understand the risks," I said, remembering the speech my father gave before we left Gasmere. He clearly explained the risks that could come and allowed everyone the chance to change their minds.

"Bring them through the Merchant's entrance. I'll meet you there in an hour."

"We'll be there. Thank you." My eyes brimmed with unshed tears.

His face softened as he looked at me. "We may be in scary times, but that doesn't mean we can't extend help." He moved his focus to Gil. "Please be discreet as you leave. The guards will be on patrol."

"Thank you for the warning," he said, placing his hood over his head.

The Elder opened the door a sliver and looked through the gap before giving us a nod of his head. "Best of luck," he said, opening it fully.

I lifted my hood and followed Gil out. I couldn't help but feel this new sense of hope stir inside of me.

CHAPTER 24

Talia

"Again," I said, then wiped the sweat from my eye.

Adira advanced slowly. I observed her every motion, mentally rehearsing the defensive techniques they had taught me. She stepped her dominant foot forward and twisted her hips slightly, which was a sign she was about to attack.

I dodged her fist by shifting to the side, which forced her to readjust.

"Well done," Hafsa cheered from the side. "Now control the distance."

Staying light on my toes, I faced Adira as she moved back and forth before me, trying to throw me off. She inched closer, and I gradually moved backward to distance myself. Every part of me wanted to throw a punch, but I was supposed to be on defense.

I saw her left fist approaching my cheek from the corner of my eye. I leaned back, but she was too fast. She advanced, dropping her left fist and using her right to deliver a blow to my stomach. I hunched over, having lost my breath—a mistake. Adira seized my shoulders and swung her foot behind mine, exerting a force that sent me crashing onto the ground.

I stayed there, squinting up at the sun. It was noon and the air was warm, but it was still the only time we could train. However, that would change after today.

"You lasted longer that time." Adira stood over me and extended her hand. I groaned as she helped me stand. "You're in your head too much."

"That's because I don't know what I'm doing. Everything feels awkward and foreign," I said, then accepted the water Hafsa handed to me.

"It will come," Hafsa said, offering a sympathetic smile. "The more you practice, the more your body will remember the movements and react more naturally."

"Sure." I handed the canteen back. I chose not to share my true source of annoyance, which was that the deal would expire in two days, and my fighting was nowhere near sufficient enough to protect my parents or myself from King Madden and his men. Every morning I woke hoping my parents would show up in Aydencia, but I had an ominous feeling that if I wanted to find them, I would have to be the one to go searching.

"Again," I said, pushing my braid behind me and walking back into the ring. Adira opened her mouth and then looked over at Hafsa. "You said I needed more practice."

"Yes, but that comes with time…" Hafsa said.

"Your Highness!"

I snapped toward the voice. Nadav ran in our direction, and my chest deflated because I thought it was someone else. Someone who hadn't shown up to the training session, not like he did anything but stare from the sidelines anyways. I had a feeling he was avoiding me. He hadn't said a word to me since our moment by the tree. Not even at the special dinners they orchestrated for the "lost princess", when he was seated next to me.

"Your Highness." Nadav stopped in front of me. I bit the inside of my lower lip, trying to school my face. "Alon is requesting an audience with you before the festivities start."

My eyes widened. "Is it about my parents? Has he heard something?"

"Not that I know of," Nadav said, throwing a side-glance at Hafsa.

"Tell him I'll stop by after training." I lifted my fists facing Adira, pushing past the disappointment.

She shook her head and pointed toward the sun. "Training is over."

I shielded my eyes and glanced at the sun's position. Dropping my hand, I looked back at Nadav annoyed. "I'll head there now."

"We'll come," Hafsa offered.

"No," I said, walking toward my cloak. "I'd rather have some time alone." The cloak clung to my warm skin, making me feel more uncomfortable. The announcement of my identity would have one advantage. I would no longer need to travel in the shadows. However, I wasn't sure being paraded around the city for people to gawk at was worth it. Although they said I wasn't a prisoner, it all felt the same as at the palace, constantly being used to further someone else's agenda. If given the choice, I would embrace a life within the confines of this cloak hidden from everyone.

I made my way to Skyhall, taking the quickest route possible and keeping my face hidden. A part of me couldn't help but hope that maybe, just maybe, Alon had news about my parents. I trusted that he hadn't heard anything and wasn't lying to me, again. I clenched my fists as I walked up the stairs to the doors of Skyhall. Raph had taken me to Alon's study after he found me by the Remembrance Tree so Alon could explain what I had overheard. But his reasoning still didn't excuse his actions, regardless if he thought it was for the greater good. He intentionally let me walk straight into the king's hands. I didn't care if he said he wasn't positive that I was the "lost princess".

He knew what King Madden was doing with those young women.

He did nothing to warn the people of Landore.

He let it all happen.

Sure, he saved some of them, but not all. I ground my teeth thinking about the young women I saw during my first meeting with King Madden. As I stopped in front of Alon's door, I tried to prepare myself for whatever I might learn next.

I knocked twice.

"Please, come in." Alon's voice was gentle. When I entered, he was standing by his desk. "Thank you for coming so quickly, Your Highness." I rocked onto my heels. "Take a seat."

"I'd rather stand," I said.

"I wanted to make sure you were ready for this evening."

"You don't have to worry. I've had training on how to be a princess," I replied, letting the anger I felt engulf my words.

His eyes saddened. "I know I've hurt you, but—"

"We've been through this, and I'd rather not talk about it again."

"As you wish." I felt regret radiate from him, but I still wasn't in a place to forgive him. He'd hurt me and those I love even if he said it was unintentional.

"Is that all?"

"I have one more thing," he answered, shifting his gaze to his desk. "It's the only thing left we have from your...from those we believe to be your birth parents." He walked behind his desk, but his hand froze next to a drawer. "I know you don't believe they were your biological parents, but I still believe this should belong to you." He opened the drawer and retrieved a small package wrapped in brown paper. He extended it out for me to grab. "Please," he said, obviously sensing my reluctance.

I snatched the package and tucked it inside my waistband.

"I better go get ready. We wouldn't want the 'lost princess' to be late to her parade," I said, turning to leave.

Alon let me walk out the door without another word. The entire way back to my room, I could feel the weight of the package. Once inside, I took it out of my waistband and dropped it on the bed as if it was a hot coal. I didn't owe Alon or the late princess and her husband anything. But without fully understanding why, I reached out to grab the small, brown package.

I opened it and an item slipped out. I barely caught it by its golden chain. It was a necklace with a large circular pendant. I flipped it over. There was a gold tree carved in the middle of it. It resembled the Remembrance Tree with its wide trunk and many branches. I rubbed the tree with my thumb, thinking about the moment Raph and I shared.

Behind the tree was some sort of onyx stone that glistened in the light. A gold border with intricate designs circled the outside. It was beautiful. I flipped it around, but there were no engravings on it. I slipped it over my neck and went to wash up. It was just a necklace, and I needed a new one anyway.

"What is that?" I asked, disgusted. An open carriage, pulled by two white horses, was parked in front of me. The exterior was adorned with garlands of deep green and large, brightly colored flowers.

"You didn't think they would let the lost princess make her debut without a grand entrance, did you?" Adira whispered in my ear with an air of laughter.

"I'm not riding in that," I said. Richard had his hand extended to help me into the carriage. I felt awkward enough in the frilly pink dress they had me wearing.

"A lot of time and effort went into planning this, and we are already late." He emphasized this point by placing his hand back out.

Giving an audible exhale, I accepted his help into the carriage. Adira followed me, and having her next to me was the only comfort I had. I eyed her outfit with envy. I had come to know it as the uniform Aydencian warriors wore, and I would have sworn off eating sweets for a whole season if I could have worn one instead of the pink monstrosity I had on.

"Okay." Adira's father was the last one to sit. He and Hanna were sitting across from us in outfits that were similar in style to mine. "We will make our way through the city by going down to the pier where we'll do a formal introduction of you to the people," he said, as if the plan hadn't been explained to me countless times already. "Driver, I think we are read—wait! Where is Raph?" he asked.

"Why does—" I started.

"I'm right here." Raph jogged down the stairs and came to stand right next to me outside the carriage. It didn't take me long to realize Eitan, who stood on the opposite side, and him were placed as guards. "Sorry, Richard. I had to finish something for Alon." He glanced up at me from the corner of his eye.

"Fine. Fine." Richard waved his hand and sat. "Driver," he called out, and the carriage lunged forward with a snap.

The journey down the mountain took longer than usual, even by horse. We had to take an indirect way to avoid the stairs, and my back ached from the continual bouncing from the uneven paths. Raph's eyes flicked in my direction every other minute, but I couldn't tell if it was out of duty or something more.

The carriage crawled as we approached the trade buildings where the crowds were formed. A little girl ran to the carriage with a flower in her small, out-stretched hand. "For Princess Talia," she said with an enormous grin on her sun-kissed face.

"Uh, thank you," I said, accepting the flower but unable to hide the shock on my face.

"You are going to have to do better than that," Richard whispered across the carriage.

Plastering a smile on my face, I waved as we passed the people. The majority cheered and clapped, but there were a few who stood further back with skepticism on their faces. I tightened my grip around the flower stem.

By the time we reached the water, my cheeks burned and my lap was filled with flowers and gifts.

"Stop," Richard said to the driver as we pulled in front of a platform by the water.

We came to a halt, and the crowd pushed forward and surrounded the carriage. Alon stepped out from the crowd and placed his hands out in front of him to keep the people from coming any further. He then took position opposite Raph on the other side of the carriage door.

Richard dipped his head toward the platform.

"Right." I stood, which caused the gifts to fall to my feet. "Should I…"

"Leave them," Hanna said with a smile.

Raph reached toward me. I grabbed his hand, reminded of the intimate moment we shared days ago. He said nothing nor even looked at me as he helped me down. I retracted my hand from his the moment my feet touched the ground. His obvious resentment of what happened between us hurt enough, I didn't need to punish myself more by the comfort of his touch.

The crowd screamed my name, vying for my attention. Their faces were filled with excitement, which caused the knot in my stomach to tighten. I couldn't do this. I took a slight step back, bringing my hand to my chest where the necklace was hidden under the dress, but I couldn't reach it. The collar of the dress came all the way to my neck.

I inhaled sharply as warmth wrapped around my other hand.

Raph's eyes were soft and almost had a look of concern, as if he knew there was a storm of anxiety inside of me. I stared at our hands, unable to understand how his touch was able to calm me and why I wasn't moving away from him. His hand tightened around mine, and I looked back into those dangerous green eyes. He placed my hand in the crook of his arm and lifted one side of his mouth. I hated how much he was comforting me, yet I couldn't pull away. I needed it.

He escorted me up the platform where the four other leaders of Aydencia, who I met during that catastrophe of a dinner, were standing on the platform. If I had to guess, it was a bid to show their support of the claim that I was the lost princess. Raph brought me to the middle and then positioned himself behind me next to Adira and Eitan. The peace I had felt vanished as Alon came to one side of me and Richard and Hanna on the other. Taking a deep breath, I convinced myself that I could do this. I had survived King Madden and I would survive this.

The crowd quieted as Richard stepped forward.

"My dear Aydencians, you have all heard the rumors circling Landore that Madden had found the lost princess." A chorus of boos trickled through the crowd. "I'm here to confirm they were true. He discovered the daughter of Princess Adeline and Jaxon. However, four of our bravest warriors infiltrated Madden's palace and saved her," he said, grabbing a fist full of air.

Excited shouts echoed throughout the space.

I dropped my chin, unsure of what I was hearing. I helped Raph escape. Catherine, Malenee, and I did that. It wasn't the other way around.

"And she stands before you today. Our lost princess, Princess Talia Breon." Richard stepped to the side and gestured for me to come forward. The people cheered.

Clasping my hands in front of me, I offered my best regal smile and stepped next to Richard. My smile slipped as I scanned the crowd. They were staring at me like I was the answer they had been waiting for, like I was their salvation. I took a small step back, but then forced my feet to stay rooted where they were.

"You have been the symbol of hope for many of these people for years," Hanna whispered as she came to stand on my other side. My eyes landed on an older couple. They were holding each other with tears in their eyes. "They've hoped that once the lost princess was found, they could go back home."

I swallowed past the lump in my throat when they broke into a wide grin as they realized I was staring at them. I shifted my focus.

"How can we trust she's the daughter of Princess Adeline?" A loud voice called out and the crowd went silent. "What if she's working with Madden?"

"To lead him straight to us!" A fearful voice yelled from the opposite direction.

My mouth opened, but Richard quickly stepped next to me placing his hand on my back.

"Aydencians, Her Highness was held as a prisoner by Madden and endured his cruelty. Even at this very moment he plots to harm those she cares about. Rest assured, Her Highness holds no allegiance to him."

Richard guided me off the stage. People resumed their cheers and the chanting of my name, but there was an odd feeling in the air. As if many were still un-convinced by Richard's words. We slowly made our way back to the carriage, but not before Richard took every opportunity to introduce me to prominent figures of Aydencia. Among them were the city's equivalent to a Head Healer, the Port Master, and a man who had been a distant relation to the royal family.

"Your Highness, this is Professor Jethro." Richard ges-tured to an older gentleman with gray shoulder-length hair that blended into a full gray beard. "He teaches history to the students here at The Academy."

"It is such an honor, Your Highness," the professor said while bowing. He wore a long robe and reminded me of what I always pictured a wise old man to look like.

I shuffled, unsure if I would ever get used to strangers bowing to me. "It's a pleasure, Professor."

"Jethro was your mother's tutor in the palace," Richard added.

"Oh." Was all I had to say.

His voice shook as he talked. "I tutored all three of the king and queen's children." He lifted his chin.

"Well, The Academy is very fortunate to have someone like you as a teacher," I said, focused on keeping my voice light.

"Teaching is my life's passion. I'm grateful to do it anywhere." His hand shook as he lifted it to run his fingers through his beard. "Please know, Your Highness, that my door is always open to you." His eyes were filled with warmth, which melted a part of my facade.

"Thank you. Maybe I will take you up on that offer. I'm afraid I was taught very little truth about Landore's history." If I had planned on staying in Aydencia, I would have taken advantage of his offer. My time spent in the king's library was one of the things that kept me sane. I had grown a love for reading and learning about Landore and the other kingdoms. Knowledge I believed every Landorian should have access to.

"I would be honored, Your Highness." He gave another bow before turning to Richard and dismissing himself.

As we approached the carriage, I paused to look over the numerous knarves docked nearby. On the closest pier, a group of young sailors stood with their eyes fixed on me. I raised my hand to wave. The young sailors responded with beaming smiles and playfully nudged each other. Returning their smiles, I considered it might be wise to befriend some sailors in case Raph failed to hold up his end of the deal.

As if on cue, Raph stepped in front of me, blocking the sailors from my view.

"Your Highness," he said, extending his hand.

I grabbed my skirts and stepped into the carriage by myself. Without all that anxiety coursing through me I could think straight again. I was done being thrown around by Raph's constant change of emotions.

"I think that went well," Richard said as the carriage took off. "Wonderful job, Your Highness."

"Are you serious? What about what those people shouted?" I asked, unable to let their concerns go. I didn't blame them for voicing their fears. They had the right to question my motives. They didn't know me.

"Don't worry, they just need time to accept it all. Announcing the lost princess will change many things for our people," Richard said with a wide smile.

I grimaced, not able to share his confidence that everyone would accept it with time. However, it might not matter. For if my parents didn't show in two days, I wouldn't be here to be their lost princess.

As we left the crowds and ascended the mountain, I dared a glance over my shoulder, expecting to see a certain pair of green eyes, but an unfamiliar face stared back at me. A man wearing a warrior uniform walked along my side of the carriage, but it was not Raph. I had never seen him before. I turned to Adira.

"I don't know," she mouthed and shrugged.

I placed my hands in my lap, determined to not worry about where Raph could be.

When we arrived back at Skyhall, the sun had already set. All I thought about was crawling into bed and leaving the day behind me.

I walked toward my room and began removing the pins in my updo. I struggled with one particularly stubborn pin as the door behind me latched shut. I took a couple of steps toward the bed, but saw a figure by the fireplace.

A scream tore through me and the pins fell to the floor.

The figure was next to me in seconds.

"Shh." Raph lifted his hand to cover my mouth.

I clutched at my heart and took a few steps back. "What are you doing here?"

He stared at me, then paced in front of me.

"What are you doing in *my* room?"

One of his hands combed through his hair as his gaze stayed fixed on me, but he didn't stop pacing.

"Raph!"

In three steps, he stood a breath away.

"I heard word of your parents."

"What?" I asked, blinking.
"Pack your things. We're leaving tonight."

Chapter 25

Kasper

THE SMELL OF SMOKE drifted into my tent as Sal opened the flap and sauntered in. "Report," I commanded as I stared at the map.

"The eastern side of the village, which I believe was the Merchants', has been laid to waste," he answered with a satisfied smirk. He relished in the fact that I had given him more control. After my run-in with the rebels, something needed to change. I ordered Sal to instill more fear in the villagers, but he had the freedom to do it in his own way.

"And what of the villagers?" I asked, unconcerned by the damage they inflicted.

"No one's saying anything yet, but when the new recruits join, we will have more men at our disposal to help with interrogations."

"We need answers *now*." I ground my teeth as the map beneath my hands became a blur. Trying to control my rage, I released my breath. But it did nothing. My control had gotten worse over the past two days, since I lost those rebels. It needed to be released.

"We could start kidnapping again, Your Highness."

My head snapped up at Sal's suggestion. He pulled back from me. "It worked last time," he said, less sure of himself.

"Did it? From what I remember, it ended with all of us tied up in the back of a wagon," I seethed while walking around the table. "All because you couldn't smell out a rebel in your midst." I grimaced, hiding the pain from my injured leg, yet not stopping my advancement.

"Yes...well..." His eyes darted to the entrance of the tent. "In the end, we were able to flush out the lost princess."

"Because we got an anonymous tip that someone had missed their calling ceremony. It was by chance!" My face was inches from his. I was doing everything in my power not to allow the rage to pour out of me.

"Your Highness!" Oliver called into the tent. The chill from the night air slipped in. "We," his voice lowered when he fully entered, "have found a traveling Merchant in the village who the villagers say might know something. They say he's been spouting stories about knowing the lost princess."

I released Sal from my stare. "Bring him to me," I commanded Oliver. "You're dismissed." I waved at Sal as I turned around.

I moved back to the table and allowed it to take some of my weight as I exhaled. No one knew of my injury, and I planned it to stay that way. There was no way I could show weakness, especially in front of Sal. My eyes drifted back down to the map. We were in the northernmost village in Landore before Llycia. I needed a lead. There wasn't another choice.

"I'll tell you any story you want to hear," a muffled voice said from outside. "You don't have to be so forceful." The voice grunted as it got closer.

"Oof." An older man fell into my tent and landed on his knees. Sal walked in next, followed by Oliver.

"This is the traveling Merchant, Your Highness," Oliver said.

"Your Highness?" The man stood and locked eyes with me. "Oh," he said, his eyes widening before a small smile pulled at his lips. "This will be a good story."

"What's your name?" I asked.

"Pete. But I'm known as Crazy Old Pete to many of the villagers." His smiled widened and he pulled his shoulders back slightly with what seemed like pride.

"And you know who I am?"

"Of course, Your Highness," he answered with a dip of his head.

"And my reputation?"

His throat bobbed. "Yes…"

"Great. Now that we know each other, let's get to the reason I brought you here." I leaned against the front of the table and crossed my arms. "Rumors are floating around that you know Princess Talia personally." I raised an eyebrow. "Is this true?"

He laughed awkwardly while rubbing the back of his neck. "I have never talked with her with that title. I knew her as the outcast from Gasmere. But I will say, she loved to listen to my stories." He stared off into the corner of the tent with a faint smile on his lips. I followed his gaze, but nothing was there. Something was definitely off about him.

"And her parents?" I asked, gaining his attention again.

"Aye, I knew them too. Not personally, just of them. In a profession like mine, you come to know many people." He shrugged and gave a wary look back at Sal and Oliver.

I pushed off the table and exhaled. This man was testing my sanity. "And have you come across her parents recently?"

"I heard you were looking for them, going village to village in search of them and those rebels." He scanned the tent, taking in the different items.

"And?" I asked through my teeth.

"Haven't seen them since the last time I was in Gasmere." He shrugged. "That would have been before the Harvest Festival, I believe…"

My hand wrapped around his tunic, and I pulled him close. His mouth opened and his eyes doubled in size. "I'm going to let you in on a little secret," I said, dropping my voice. "I'm quite desperate at the moment, and you are the only lead I have." I tightened my grip on his shirt. "And every word you have said so far has made me want to end your miserable life." Unsheathing the dagger strapped to my chest, I pressed it against his neck. "So, let's try this again."

He nodded ever so slightly.

"Have you come across any suspicious individuals recently? Maybe ones that carry characteristics from another kingdom?" I asked. "And think hard before you speak." I pressed the dagger, leaving a small crimson line across his neck.

"No, Your Highness." His voice trembled.

This couldn't be all he knew. Because if I didn't find Talia or her parents soon… The rage sparked to life inside of me, thinking about what my father was doing to Lliana. "That's too bad," I said, moving my arm across my chest, prepared to release a quick slash against his frail skin.

"Wait!" He croaked out.

I cocked my head.

"There...there...was a man." Dropping the dagger to my side, I released my grip on his tunic by a fraction. "He asked for directions to the nearest village, which wasn't that strange. I get asked that a lot." I lifted the dagger. "But...but there were two others with him. And the whole time the man talked with me, they kept their hoods up and heads down without a word."

I released my grip and pushed him toward Oliver, who wrapped his hands around the man's arms.

"Where were they headed?" I asked, walking over to the map.

"He asked for directions to the nearest coastal village in the west. I pointed him toward Banesmyth."

Placing my finger against the village on the map, I let the tension roll off me.

"Sal, tell the men we head out in the hour," I ordered.

"Yes, Your Highness," he said, then exited the tent.

"What would you like me to do with him, sir?" Oliver asked, still holding the man by his arms.

"We'll take him with us. I'd hate to travel all that way to find out he was lying to me."

The man was finally rendered speechless as his throat bobbed.

"Take him away," I said, waving Oliver out of the tent.

"It's time to find some rebels," I muttered under my breath while placing a pin next to Banesmyth.

CHAPTER 26

Raph

"WHY DO I FEEL like no one knows we are doing this?" Talia whispered behind me.

I checked the area, then motioned for her to follow me out of the shadows from a building and onto the main street. No one was around, but the moon was full and gave enough light for anyone to see us.

"Hurry," I said, increasing my speed. I heard an exasperated sigh, but also the sound of quickened feet. I ducked behind a couple of barrels as we approached the docks.

Talia bent beside me. "Are you going to tell me why we are sneaking around? Does Alon know about this?"

"No," I said, peering out for signs of anyone on the docks, but everything was quiet and still. Many of the people continued to celebrate the announcement of the lost princess with drinks, leaving the streets abandoned at this early hour.

"No you will not tell me, or no Alon doesn't know?"

I whipped my head in her direction. "Princess, can we talk about this when we are safely out of Aydencia?"

She pursed her lips and then nodded.

"Great, follow me."

I ran toward a knarve at the end of the dock. I pulled myself over the edge and reached down to help Talia. She stared at me with a quizzical look.

"Why don't we take that smaller one over there?" she asked. It was the same one she tried to use to run away.

"Please trust me," I said, extending my hand, trying to get my eyes to convey the urgency I felt. She positioned her foot in a worn-out hold and grasped my outstretched hand.

I lifted her into the knarve. The creaking wood reverberated through the air. I held my breath as I surveyed our surroundings. But everything was still, outside the rhythmic sway of the knarve beneath us. I turned to work on the ropes, but Talia stood in front of me with her arms crossed.

"I need some answers. How am I to believe you are truly taking me to find my parents and not somewhere else?"

As I forced the air out of my nose, I grabbed her arm and brought her to the other end of the knarve, where someone was less likely to see us. "No, Alon doesn't know we are leaving, so we have to sneak around. We can't take the smaller vessel because it's not one of ours. Nadav and Hafsa came here on it, and I'm not confident enough to sail it alone," I said in one breath. "Any other questions?" I peered over my shoulder. I couldn't shake the feeling that someone was watching.

"Yes." She pulled her arm away. "Why doesn't Alon know what we are doing? How did you find out about my parents if he didn't tell you?"

I pushed my hair back, wishing she would wait until we were safely out of Aydencia to ask these questions. Someone could have already noticed she was missing. "Before the parade, I was in Alon's study submitting some paperwork, and I noticed a letter on his desk. It requested a ship for three passengers as soon as possible. It stated they had precious cargo that needed to be transported to safety." Her face scrunched together and then she opened her mouth to speak, but I cut her off. "It's your parents. Trust me."

"You expect me to trust you, after you haven't spoken to me in days?"

A sharp pain went straight through my heart. Her eyes narrowed, but I could see the hurt I had caused her in them. I thought distance would be the best thing for both of us, seeing I had allowed my feelings to get the best of me. I couldn't get more involved with her than

I already was. It had been physically painful for me to try to shut off my emotions toward her, but I deserved to feel that pain. I wasn't good enough for her. She was a princess, and I was no one. But I never thought for a second I was hurting her. I bit down on my tongue. I never did anything right when it came to her.

"I'm sorry. I wasn't trying to betray your trust," I said.

"Then what were you doing?" Her lips pressed into a thin line as if she regretted asking the question.

"I..." I frantically searched for a plausible reason for my actions. "I was trying to give you some space. I thought you would need some time to process through everything."

Her eyebrows furrowed. "And what about not being at training?"

"I had other things to handle," I said cryptically. It wasn't a lie though. I was investigating the reason behind Hafsa and Nadav still being here, and what they wanted from Talia. I planned to tell her if I had found anything, but I didn't.

Her shoulders dropped. "Did the letter state where they are?"

"They are waiting near the coastal village of Banes-myth," I answered, thankful for the change in subject. "Unfortunately, it is on the other side of Landore. It will take us four days to get there."

"Okay," she said, moving closer to me. "But why are you doing this?" She took another step. "Why are you going behind Alon's back?"

My gut tightened at her closeness, her chest mere inches from mine. She looked at me expectantly as if she could tell I was withholding something from her. But I couldn't tell her how I was doing this for her, because that would only make things worse. "Because..." I rubbed at the back of my neck and decided to go with a different truth. "Because I'm not sure when Alon received that letter, and I don't know if he will hold up his end of your deal. He hasn't been fully forthcoming with me," I confessed under my breath. "Plus, I made you a promise, and I intend to keep it."

She moved closer, leaning into me. The soft brush of her lips kissed my cheek. I swallowed, trying to quench my dry mouth as she slowly pulled away. "Thank you," she said, biting her lower lip. The lip I could still feel on my cheek like a hot iron.

There was a moment of stillness where neither of us moved. My mind wandered back to the Remembrance Tree and the intense desires that still raged within me. The ones I needed to silence, but she was making it near impossible to do so.

Not fully aware of my actions, my hand lifted toward her face. My thumb gently touched her bottom lip, releasing it from between her teeth.

Her chest compressed as air escaped from her mouth. My eyes stayed on her parted lips. The same lips I had thought of kissing for months.

In one movement, I wrapped my hand around the back of her neck and brought her into me. Her lips met mine and the small amount of control I had vanished. I felt her body tense but then as quickly press into me. Warmth traveled throughout my whole body as her soft lips responded with the same desperation I felt. Her hands traveled up my back, and I buried my hand deeper into her hair, never wanting to let her go. Never wanting this kiss to end. But it had to. A small voice in my head broke through my overwhelming desire.

I dropped my hand and pulled away. She leaned into to me, her eyes still closed. It took everything inside of me not to kiss her again.

"I can't," I said slightly out of breath. "I can't do this with *you*."

Hurt painted across her face.

I slammed my teeth together wanting to punch myself for being so stupid with my words.

"Right," she said, wiping the emotion from her face.

"Talia, what I—"

The creaking of the floorboards near the front of the knarve pulled my attention. I narrowed my eyes over Talia's shoulder.

"No. You're right. It was a mistake. Let's just forget about it." Pink painted across her cheeks.

I opened my mouth to try to explain, but my mind was still focused on the sound I heard. I had this feeling we weren't alone.

She took a step away from me and looked around, rubbing her arm. "Are you sure we can sail this by ourselves?"

"Of course you can't." Talia jumped at the unannounced voice.

Adira emerged from the shadows with Eitan who landed on the knarve with a resounding thud.

"We're hurt you'd try without us," Eitan said.

I shook my head. Not surprised by their presence since I knew someone was out there, but annoyed by their timing. The pink tinge on Talia's cheeks darkened.

"We'd better hurry. I heard you a mile away," Adira said with a smirk, untying the knarve from the dock.

I looked back to Talia, but her focus was on the knarve's floorboards. I would have to wait to explain myself to her. Rolling my shoulders back, I focused on the task ahead of us. "Eitan, take the helm," I ordered. "I'll man the sails, and Princess, get ready to see your parents again."

CHAPTER 27

Jules

"WHAT ARE WE GOING to do?" I asked Gil as I dropped my head into my hands. I stared blankly at the stained table.

"We will figure it out. We can't give up."

"This is the third village that has turned us down in the past five days since Hattlee. No one is taking them in." I squeezed my eyes shut, not allowing myself to imagine the four families' faces when we told them the news.

"You don't know that. And the owner didn't turn us away for the same reason as the other two villages. He just has no available rooms."

We arrived in the coastal village, Banesmyth, as dawn approached, and went straight to the tavern to talk with the owner. After he informed us of having no rooms, we grabbed an empty table to figure out our next move. There were a handful of others in the tavern who were mostly eating. I looked up as an older man walked past our table.

"Yes, but you saw his face." I leaned forward and lowered my voice. "Word has spread about what happened to the other villages." My blood boiled thinking about it. "They're scared."

"That doesn't mean there aren't people willing to help," Gil said, his amber eyes shining with hope under his hood. I couldn't help but wonder how we could see things so differently. "The other villages we tried were dealing with the aftermath of those fires. It doesn't seem like the prince has visited this village yet." He peered over his shoulder as he finished.

Sighing, I allowed my body to sag. "Let's try to find an Elder to talk—"

"Excuse me." I startled at the deep voice behind me.

It was the older man who had walked past moments prior.

"I didn't mean to scare you, miss. I overheard you mentioning you need some rooms." I widened my eyes at Gil, wondering how much this man had heard of our conversation. "My companions and I are moving on this morning, which leaves two rooms vacant. I already talked with the owner, so if you want them, they're yours."

"Really?" I looked from the man to Gil. I expected to see a smirk on his face, implying I needed to have more faith. Instead, his eyes narrowed as he observed the stranger.

"You don't have to take them if you don't want them," the man said, giving Gil a skeptical look.

"We will take them. Thank you," I said.

He dipped his head. "Talk to the owner about the keys," he said and walked away.

Gil's attention stayed with the man as he walked to a back table where two others were sitting.

"What's wrong?" I whispered.

"I think I know him. I just can't place from where," he said, peering over his shoulder one more time at the man.

"Maybe you crossed paths when you were searching for the kidnappers?"

He shook his head.

I leaned over to look around Gil at their table. The other two, with the older man, had their hoods up, concealing their faces. One of them raised their drink, and the light illuminated their face.

My mouth dropped open. I had known that face for most of my life.

"It's them," I said, pushing up from the chair.

"Who?" Gil whipped his head back and forth.

My throat tightened. "Tal's parents," I choked out.

I made my way to the table, and the older man stood. Laurel placed her hand on her husband's arm.

"Jules," they said at the same time.

"What are you doing here?" Laurel asked.

"Me? You are the ones that are supposed to be in Aydenc—"

"Why don't you take a seat, and we can discuss this quietly," the older man said, extending his hand to the two empty chairs at their table.

I wasn't sure when Gil joined me, but he pulled out one chair for me and then sat in the other one. After we were seated, I leaned across the table toward Laurel. "Tals was on her way to Ay—"

"Mhm." The older man tilted his head while raising his brow.

"She was on her way to find you two. Why are you still here?"

Laurel looked at John, and then they looked at the older man.

"We have been trying to get transport, but it's been difficult to say the least," he answered.

"What do you mean?" Gil uncrossed his arms but didn't remove his focus from the man.

"Do we know each other?" the man asked.

"I was going to ask you the same thing."

They locked eyes and then the man clasped his fingers together in front of his chest and gave them a shake along with a nod of his head. Gil's mouth spread into a wide grin as he copied the same move. They reached across the table and shook forearms.

"I knew you were familiar," Gil said. "Name's Gil."

"Trenton," he said with a bow of his head. "Wait, Richard and Hanna's boy?"

"The one and only." Gil smirked and dipped his head.

"Wow, you've grown up."

"How long have you been on mission?" Gil asked as Tal's parents and I tried to follow their conversation.

Trenton rubbed his chin. "It's been a while. Over five years now."

"Where were you stationed?"

"Llycia. My boy got in as a gardener at the palace." Trenton's face fell. "Until...well, one day he didn't come home."

My heart sank as I watched him grieve his son. Gil placed his hand over his heart. "I'm sorry."

"It's why I volunteered when Gale asked for a transporter. I couldn't stay in the city, being constantly reminded of him. Plus," he looked over at Tal's parents, "reuniting parents with their daughter, especially the lost princess, seemed like the perfect mission to honor my Felix."

A moment of silence passed between us.

"What about you two?" Trenton asked.

"I'm sure you've heard about the fires?" I asked, and they nodded their heads. "Gasmere was destroyed. Nothing was left standing, except for the Meeting House. We were running out of food and places for people to stay for the winter." Laurel clutched at John, and he wrapped his arm around her. "So, my parents sent out groups of volunteers to find refuge, but it hasn't been that easy." I peered at Gil.

"Other villages are scared. The prince has been applying pressure on them to find you two," Gil said, gesturing to Tal's parents with his head.

"That's why we've been on the move," John said.

"We've been moving from one rendezvous spot to the next, waiting for transport, but none has come." Trenton looked at Gil as if he had the answer, but Gil rubbed his chin with a furrowed brow. "I sent another correspondence four days ago, and we are heading to the rendezvous spot this morning."

"Strange..." Gil said.

"I'm glad to know you both are alright," I said to Tal's parents. "I'm sure Talia is going crazy, not knowing where you are." The knots in my stomach tightened at the guilt of failing to keep my first promise to watch out for her parents. "But now that we have found a place for the remaining families," I turned to Gil, "maybe we can escort them to the next location?"

Gil easily accepted my proposition. "We will journey with you as added protection but also to find out why there has been no transportation sent yet."

"Thank you," Trenton said.

"We will meet you outside the village entrance in an hour," Gil said.

I followed his lead but turned back to Laurel and John. "We will get you to Tals."

I could barely see Trenton through the thick layer of fog. We were traveling north from Banesmyth and using the trees surrounding the coastline as coverage. Apparently, there was a rendezvous spot that the Northern Rebels used nearby. Then we would hopefully get transport to Aydencia for Tal's parents.

Gil walked next to me as we stayed behind the other three. We hadn't said anything to one another since leaving the village. My fingers played with the fabric of my cloak as I glanced over at him. I opened my mouth to close it a second later.

"What is it?" Gil asked when I glanced over for a second time.

"Nothing."

He lowered his head toward me.

"Well, I was thinking that it would make sense for you to join them back to Aydencia, if that's what you want. Especially since transportation seems hard to come by. And I...I mean, those villagers you've helped will forever be grateful. You've done more than enough for Gasmere," I finished, focusing my attention straight ahead. I had said what I needed to say, but I felt worse for it. I knew Gil wanted to return to Aydencia. He had spent the first hour of this journey talking animatedly with Trenton about all the great things in Aydencia.

The back of my neck burned as I felt Gil's gaze on me. "Look at me," he said in a low voice. I caught his stare. "I'm not going anywhere. I made a promise to Talia to keep you safe, and in my eyes, that doesn't end until you two are reunited. Sorry, but you're stuck with me." He winked and then nudged me with his shoulder.

The heat from my neck traveled to my cheeks as I tried to suppress a smile. I wanted to say more, but I couldn't find the words. Men always flirted with me and vied for my attention, but I never felt anything from it. Mainly because they had an ulterior motive: to take advantage of the influence my family had in Gasmere. Gil was different. It was like he saw me for me, not for who my parents were or what he could gain from me. It was making my body react in ways I had never experienced before.

Trenton's hand raised and we halted, then slowly approached him.

"What is it?" Gil asked, peering into the fog.

"I thought I saw someone," Trenton whispered, reaching for the short sword attached to his hip.

Everyone stilled, scanning the area.

Taking a small step forward, I narrowed my eyes. The fog was so thick that anyone could be hiding in it. My breath hitched as the tree in front of me appeared to move. I kept my eyes on it as I slowly lifted my hand to grab my bow.

I heard a sharp inhale behind me.

"Run!" Gil yelled as red figures emerged from the fog.

CHAPTER 28

Kasper

"I WANT THEM ALIVE," I shouted, trying to get my voice to carry through the dense fog as the men went after the group we had been tracking. "You," I yelled at the closest guard. "Go inform Sal." He bowed his head and took off. With a knot of anxiety tightening in my chest, I retraced my steps to where I had left my horse. I ignored the searing pain coursing through my leg and quickened my pace.

Finally, the faint sound of a horse whinnying reached my ears. With a surge of determination, I swung myself into the saddle. As I urged the horse forward, I relinquished control and allowed him to navigate through the trees as I listened. Stomping feet and snapping twigs reached my ears from ahead. I followed the sounds as the fog dissipated around me and the trees thinned out. My heart pounded as I galloped up a hill overlooking the Cyperian Sea.

At the top, ten of my father's men were fighting against three of them. As I drew closer, I realized there were five total. The other two were standing further behind as if they were being protected. They were an older man and woman. Realization dawned on me.

I grinned as I tightened the reins and steel echoed through the air. I urged my horse to go faster, aiming straight for Princess Talia's parents.

An arrow whizzed past my face and diverted my attention momentarily. I locked eyes with a woman, but her gaze shifted as she released an arrow at Julian. He deflected it with his sword, his speed reflecting his youth and training. My focus returned to the archer.

She was the rebel from Hattlee, and the blond man was still with her. They fought side by side. She released arrows as he kept the guards at bay with his swordsmanship. The third rebel was also holding his own with a sword, but they were outnumbered even with the majority of the men back at camp.

I dismounted at the same time that my father's men surrounded them. I nodded at Oliver, and walked into the circle. The rebels protecting Princess Talia's parents had their weapons raised.

"You're a little outnumbered," I said to the woman.

She stepped toward me.

"Jules," the blond man said at the same time I raised my hand to hold off the men. Something in my mind pulled at the mention of her name, but I dismissed it.

"If you weren't such a coward, then maybe you'd even the odds," she said, stopping her advance but not lowering her bow.

"Tempting." I moved in.

"That's enough," the blond rebel said while pulling his bowstring.

"Lower your weapons and surrender. There is no way to fight your way out of this."

The older rebel shared a look with the blond one, and they lowered their weapons.

"No," the rebel woman, Jules, said with a desperate look at the blond. They shared a moment and then she turned to face me with a glare before lowering her bow.

"Wise choice," I said and then turned to Oliver. "Take their weapons and bind their wrists. We rescued the princess's parents from the rebels," I finished, peering over my shoulder at our new prisoners. But something made me do a double take.

In the distance, there was a figure running up the hill in our direction.

"Who is that?" Oliver asked next to me.

Everyone turned.

Blonde hair blew in the wind, and I couldn't believe my eyes.

"Talia, don't!" her mother cried.

CHAPTER 29

Talia

"Talia, stop!" Raph's urgent voice carried in the wind behind me. My focus remained fixed on the figures standing atop the hill. Fog had concealed them as we approached the shoreline, but as soon as we reached the rocky beach, I sprinted ahead, certain it was them.

My foot slid on the slippery grass, and my hand shot forward to regain my balance. Righting myself, I reached the top, gasping for breath. I cupped my hands to my mouth to call out to them, but my voice caught in my throat when I realized they were not alone.

Crimson figures surrounded them. "No," I said under my breath. "No!" My anger and frustration took over. I had finally found my parents and I wasn't going to let the King's Guard take them from me. Taking off at a full sprint, I didn't let my mind think of the consequences.

"Talia, don't!" Mother called as everyone turned in my direction. My determination to reach her only grew, but my arm was jerked back.

"Stop! Think about what you're doing," Raph said, dragging me back down the hill.

"I know what I'm doing! I'm saving my parents! Let me go!" I attempted to remove my arm from his grip and dug my heels into the ground.

"You can't run straight into Madden's hands again. You are too important."

"To what? The cause?" I asked, giving my arm another tug. "When will you understand? I don't care about that. I only care about my parents. If anything happens to them, I swear, I will never become your lost princess," I threatened, putting all my weight into one last pull. My arm came loose as Raph's eyes widened as he stared behind me.

"It looks like we have no choice," he said, coming in front of me.

My parents, Jules, Gil, and another man were running in our direction, but the King's Guard were not far behind them. They must have used me as a distraction to get away. "Grab your parents and get to the knarve," Raph ordered, then unsheathed his sword.

"Seriously?" Adira said with a throwing knife in each hand. Eitan was seconds behind her.

"For once, I would like it to be easy," Eitan said, unsheathing his sword.

"And what would the fun be in that?" Raph took off, and we followed.

Gil and the other man were engaged with a few guards, but Jules and my parents were running in our direction. Two guards were on their heels.

Suddenly, the guards fell to the ground holding their necks. Adira grabbed two more knives and headed toward Gil. Eitan pulled away in the direction of the other man who was fighting off three guards. I reached out to my mother. It took everything in me not to collapse into her arms as our fingers intertwined.

"Watch out!" Raph pushed me to the ground as a black blur crossed my vision.

My shoulder slammed into the ground, but the adrenaline coursing through my body covered any pain I should have felt. Mother lay next to me and Raph fought a guard on a horse, but he wasn't wearing a crimson uniform. He wore all black. My heart rate quickened, and I searched frantically for Jules and my father.

"Get to the knarve!" Raph ordered as the sound of metal hitting metal rang through the air.

I helped Mother stand by wrapping my hand in hers. "Not without my father!"

"I got him!" Jules called from the other side of Raph and the guard in black.

The guard's attention shifted when he deflected an arrow. Raph took the distraction to look back at me. "Go!"

I clenched my mother's hand tighter. The same fear I felt was in her eyes too. "They'll be right behind us." I said it to her but was trying to convince myself.

I looked back at Raph who was engaged with the guard again. However, this time, the guard focused on me, and I could clearly see his face.

Prince Kasper dipped his head in my direction.

CHAPTER 30

Jules

THE BURNING SENSATION FROM my injured palm did little to divert my attention. Every part of me was on high alert and focused on my surroundings. My fingers brushed against my jaw as I brought back another arrow. It stayed true when I released, but the King's Wraith dodged it at the last moment. However, it brought his attention to me.

His eyes narrowed as he redirected his horse to face me. A part of me took pleasure seeing his frustration.

Raph's voice echoed in the distance, and I let another arrow fly. It soared straight toward the King's Wraith's chest, but he raised his sword and deflected it. His focus shifted back to Raph, granting me a clear view of Tals and her mother sprinting down the hill. John was still by my side with his gaze fixed upon his wife and daughter.

"Let's move," I said, aware that our opportunity wouldn't last long. We maneuvered around Raph and the King's Wraith, but we weren't the only ones who noticed Tals leaving. The King's Wraith urged his horse forward, swiftly passing us. I sprinted ahead while pulling another arrow. There were only a few left, and with armor protecting the King's Wraith, I doubted my hits would slow him down.

My heart grew heavy, knowing what I needed to do.

A piercing whinny filled the air as the arrow found its mark in the horse's hindquarter. Another shot followed, striking its flank as it danced around. The horse reared up and threw the King's Wraith to the ground. He recovered, but Raph charged at him, creating another opening for us. John's ragged breathing indicated he was still behind me. I gave him a nod toward the ship, and we both took off.

I risked a glance behind me and saw Gil and Adira taking on four King's Guards. They fought in perfect synchronicity as if they could anticipate each other's every move. Next to them, Eitan and Trenton fought back-to-back against five guards. I stalled as Trenton grew sluggish.

My stomach dropped.

"No!" I called at the same moment a guard's sword went through Trenton's midsection. He fell to his knees as the guard withdrew his sword. Eitan was alone against four remaining guards, but there was no way I could reach him in time. "Gil!"

His head snapped in my direction, and I frantically gestured at Eitan fighting for his life. Gil shouted something at Adira, who then sunk a knife into the back of one of the guard's neck, giving some respite to Eitan. But they needed more help.

Tightening the grip on my bow, I stepped forward.

"Jules," Tal's father called out behind me, halting my advancement. Grinding my teeth together, I turned back around. He stood wide-eyed. "Jules..." he said with a shaky breath.

The King's Wraith stalked toward us with his sword in one hand and his whip in the other. Raph was behind him, struggling to stand.

"Move." I pushed John with my free hand. We had moments before he would be upon us. I reached for my last arrow. "Ah!" My bow flew from my hands with a snap. It landed in two pieces on the ground to my right. Fear took hold as I stood defenseless. A smug half-smile crossed the King's Wraith's face, but it vanished as Raph released a guttural scream and attacked from behind.

I turned to order John to leave, but two guards were running straight for us. I searched for a way to escape, but everyone was fighting their own battles. The two guards shared a look and closed the distance. I balled my fists, using the pain from my fresh wound to awaken my senses.

"Forget them! Get the princess!" the King's Wraith ordered between strikes with Raph.

The guards shifted course, aiming to run around us. Before I could react, John tackled the two guards to the ground. The three of them rolled down the hill.

"John!" He was lying face down, unmoving. I raced toward him, using my hands to help balance myself down the slippery descent. As I reached him, he rolled onto his back with a groan. "Are you okay?"

"I'll be fine," he said, then sat up. "The guards?"

We scoured the hill. One guard was lying still in the grass, but the other was on his feet and working his way down.

"We need to get to him before he reaches them," I said, reaching to help him stand.

With a firm grip around my forearm, his face twisted in pain. "What is it?"

"It's my ankle." He placed his weight on his right foot, only to inhale sharply. "Go without me."

"I can't leave you." I was overcome by anxiety as I watched the second guard stir.

The sound of metal striking pulled my attention upward. Raph was forcing the King's Wraith back with strike after strike, but they were tiring. For a moment I thought I saw the King's Wraith's right knee buckle. He recovered, but it reminded me of his injury.

I brought my hands to my mouth, "Raph!" His focus didn't leave the fight in front of him, but he stiffened. "His right leg!"

Raph lowered himself to the ground in a spin with one leg extending out. It hit the King's Wraith's good leg, which caused him to shift his weight onto his bad one. He yelled out as he fell to his knee, dropping his sword as he clutched his leg. Raph stood over him with both swords pointed at his throat.

"Raph!" I screamed, pointing to the two guards who had successfully made their way to the rocky beach. He looked over his shoulder to where Tals and her mother stood near the rowboat and then back at the King's Wraith.

"Fall back! Get to the knarve," Raph ordered, bringing the hilt of one sword down on the King's Wraith's head. He didn't wait to see him fall before he took off down the hill.

I breathed and then realized my situation. "We can do this. Put your arm over my shoulder." John winced, but he didn't argue. His large arm draped over my shoulders as I brought my arm around his thick waist. "One step at a time," I said as we trudged on.

The commotion behind us grew louder, but I refused to stop. We had to make it. I had to get Tals's father to safety.

"Jules!" Adira's voice carried across the wind, and soon after, I heard footsteps right behind us. "What happened?" she asked, coming alongside me.

"It's his ankle."

Gil and Eitan joined us, and relief coursed through me at seeing them unharmed. However, it was short-lived as Eitan pressed his hand against his left side where his tunic was soaked in blood.

"You two go help Raph and get on the knarve. I'll stay and help Jules," Gil said, taking John's arm and placing it around his shoulder. I moved to the other side to offer some support as Eitan and Adira ran ahead of us.

Raph was on the beach slicing his sword through the air, fighting off the two guards, but it was clear his fight with the King's Wraith had taken a lot out of him. My arm tightened around John as I watched Raph lose his ground. He needed to hold on a little longer. Adira and Eitan were almost to them.

We were close to the bottom of the hill when I heard Gil mumble under his breath as he peered over his shoulder. Guards were making their way down the hill.

"We need to move faster," he ordered.

We quickened, but it wasn't enough. They were gaining on us, and it was as if the number of guards had doubled.

We arrived at the beach as the two guards were being taken out. But no sense of relief came. An arrow flew over my head, fitting into the rocks in front of us, followed by a shower of arrows across the beach. Gil pushed us to the ground and tried to deflect the arrows from hitting us.

A line of guards stood on the hill, shooting arrows down, while more than twenty were descending the hill. They would be upon us in seconds.

Gil looked at me, and the dread I felt reflected in his eyes. There wasn't another choice. I pressed my lips together and gave him a nod, knowing I was breaking another promise to Tals.

"Go!" Gil yelled at the others, who were deflecting arrows in the rowboat waiting for us. Raph gave a single dip of his head before pushing the boat further into the water.

"No! What are you doing?" Tals screamed over the water. But I couldn't see her or the boat anymore as a circle of crimson surrounded us.

CHAPTER 31

Kasper

"Tie them up," I ordered, pacing in front of a grouping of trees. The rustling of the prisoners being dragged echoed throughout the forest.

"Can't you see he's hurt?" Jules yelled at a guard as he roughly yanked Princess Talia's father forward. He collapsed onto the ground with a groan as the guard attempted to secure him to a tree. With each step, my boots pounded into the frozen ground as I watched a guard tie Jules to a different tree nearby. She looked at me with undiluted hatred. There was something about her that kept pulling at my mind.

A snicker filled the air.

Sal leaned against a tree with a smug look on his face as he zeroed in on my injured leg. There was no hiding my limp anymore, but I couldn't care less. I used the pain to fire my fury.

A crowd formed behind me, made up of my father's guards and the new recruits that joined us a few days prior, but I ignored them, keeping my focus on the three prisoners. Yet, only one would please my father.

There would be no hiding that the princess escaped my clutches. Sal most likely already had his speech prepared to notify the king about how if he and the other guards hadn't arrived when they did, there would be no prisoners.

I rolled my shoulders and tilted my neck until it popped. I needed to turn this in my favor.

I advanced on the blond rebel. "Where are they headed?"

His lips pressed into a straight line as his eyes narrowed.

"If you stay quiet, you will not like the outcome." My voice was low as I stopped mere inches from him.

He lifted the side of his mouth.

I reached my right hand out until I felt a clump of Jules's hair and yanked it hard to the side. A cry ripped through the air, and the rebel's cockiness faltered.

His gaze shifted to her, and his face softened. I pulled her head closer to me, my hand firmly wrapped in her thick hair.

"Who are you?" I asked, keeping my attention focused solely on her, unable to understand her significance in all of this.

"I know!" a voice called from the crowd behind me. I turned, not releasing my hand. "I-I know." A young man pushed through the crowd. He straightened his uniform. I rolled my eyes. One of the new recruits. I turned back around. "Your Highness, I know who she is. More importantly, I know what she means to the princess."

The woman's eyes turned into slits as she looked at the young man.

I released my grip and faced the recruit. "Do tell..." I gestured with my hand.

"Jacob, Your Highness," he said with a clumsy bow. "Jacob Martin from Gasmere."

I lowered my chin, inclining my ear toward him. "Enlighten me."

"Her name is Jules Varnier. Her parents are Elders for the Hunters."

I flared my nostrils. "You're wasting my time," I said, ready to turn around.

"She is the princess's best friend!" He took an eager step forward. "Actually, she's her *only* friend," he said under his breath. "They are like sisters. Princess Talia would do anything for her." He took another step forward. I widened my eyes.

"And how am I supposed to know what you're saying is true and not a tactic to move up in rank?" I challenged.

A few snickers traveled through the crowd.

"It's the truth." Jacob looked at the other guards and swallowed. "Before the harvest, when those young women were going missing," I tensed, "she was among them, and Tal—Princess Talia ran away from her calling ceremony to find her. I promise, Your Highness, the princess will do anything to save her."

I lifted my chin slightly as everything fell into place. The woman against the tree was the best friend the princess had accused me of kidnapping. That's why her name sounded familiar—Jules. I could feel my lips lift slightly as I turned to face her. "Thank you. That was most insightful. Now go back with the others," I commanded.

"But—"

I threw up a hand.

"I have heard a lot about you," I said, making my way to Jules. "I feel naïve for not having put it together earlier." I could almost taste the hatred radiating off of her, something I was very familiar with. But that was what I needed. This would be enough to please my father and save Lliana. It had to be.

"Your Highness," Sal pushed off the tree he was leaning on and made his way in my direction. "Could you please enlighten me on how this is good news, considering the fact that yo—*we* lost the princess."

"Because," I said through my teeth, "not only am I handing over two people the princess cares about deeply to the king, but I will also give him the location of the rebel's camp."

"How?" he asked.

"We have a personal guide." My attention shifted to the blond rebel. "And a motivator to keep him cooperative," I finished, looking at Jules.

Her brow furrowed, but the rebel's body tensed, which confirmed my suspicions.

I stepped closer. "I warned you," I said in a whisper so only he could hear.

He pulled against his restraints.

"Pack camp. We're heading to Llycia," I ordered.

It was time to see my father.

CHAPTER 32

Raph

A GALE FILLED THE sails and propelled the knarve forward. Gripping the worn wooden knobs tightly, I forced myself to stay focused on the narrow but familiar pathway leading into Aydencia. The wind had been at our backs the whole way, as if it also wanted us to get far away from that beach.

Clenching my teeth, I replayed everything that had happened in my mind once more. I searched for the answer on how I could have done things differently or how I could have ensured the safety of everyone. Yet, she was safe, and not in Madden's hands, which I tried to convince myself was most important.

My gaze landed on her blonde hair blowing in the wind. She sat in the same spot as she had the previous three days, curled into her mother while she looked out into the distance. Her mother soothed her back. The tightness in my chest turned into a stabbing pain as I watched another tear fall down her cheek. With an exhale, I shifted my focus and saw Adira absently staring at her hands as she coiled and uncoiled the same rope. I tightened my hold on the helm, trying to soothe my turmoil.

"You did everything you could," Eitan said, coming to stand next to me as Aydencia came into view.

I peered at his side. "How bad is it?" I asked.

"You didn't have another choice. We had no chance after their reinforcements came."

"There's always another choice," I said under my breath. "But I was talking about your injury."

"It's a flesh wound," he answered with a shake of his head. "Raph, you can't put this on yourself."

"It's entirely my fault!" I spun to face him, letting go of the wheel. "I went behind Alon's back and put not only the princess's life on the line but all of yours."

"But how were you to kno—"

"It doesn't matter." I grabbed the wheel again. "I knew better. And because I listened to my heart instead of orders, a warrior lost his life and who knows what will happen to Gil, Jules, and her father!"

"Raph," Eitan hissed.

Talia was staring at me with wide eyes, but the moment I looked her way, she turned around. I blew the air out of my lungs.

"They'll be used as bait," Eitan said, then placed his hand on my shoulder. "And we will save them when that time comes."

"I'm going to lower the sails," I said before stepping away and leaving Eitan in charge of the helm. Descending the stairs, I made my way toward where the mainsail was tied. Adira followed my lead and worked on the other sail. I glanced over my shoulder and caught another glimpse of Talia. Shaking my head, I refocused on the task at hand and consciously pushed thoughts of comforting her out of my mind. I had already done enough.

As we docked, Alon stood with his hands clasped behind his back. His expression didn't change as I led the group toward him. I could feel the tension in the air around him. His eyes passed by me and went straight to Talia's mother.

"Mrs. Caffrey, it's a pleasure to have you here in Aydencia. We are preparing a room next to Her Highness's for you," Alon said with a small dip of his head.

"Who?" Mrs. Caffrey's eyes were wide as she tried to take in her surroundings, but upon Talia touching her arm, she nodded. "Right," she said with a faint smile at her daughter. "They are referring to you."

Alon bowed. "Your Highness, why don't you take your mother so you both can get cleaned up and rest? Someone will bring you food."

Talia threaded her arm through her mother's to lead her away. I took a step forward to follow, but Alon's hand pressed against my chest.

"I want to see you in my study after you're done cleaning the knarve you stole," he said, looking over my shoulder before turning around to follow Talia and her mother.

"We'll help," Eitan said, placing a hand on my shoulder as Adira occupied the spot on the other side of me.

"Eitan, Adira, come give me the report," Alon called.

They gave me a sympathetic look but followed Alon. I released the tension in my shoulders with an exhale. I deserved worse.

It was dark by the time I made it to Alon's study. My back ached and my hands were raw, but it brought a sense of calm to the anxious ball of guilt inside of me.

"Come in," Alon called from the other side of the door as soon as I stopped in front of it. I pulled my shoulders back, pushed it open, and walked straight in.

Alon stood in front of his desk and looked exactly like the warrior he was. He crossed his arms over his chest as I stopped a few feet in front of him. "Would you mind explaining to me what in Landore you were thinking?"

"Sir—"

"Do you understand the risk you injected into everything we've been doing here? All of it could have been destroyed. Did you even think of the consequences?" I opened my mouth, but he spoke again, "Or were you too blinded by your feelings for the princess?"

My throat dried up. "Sir," I said with a small cough, "I can assure you my feelings for the princess are strictly professional." The ball in my stomach tightened. "I *was* thinking about the cause. The princess would do nothing for us unless her parents were safe. We had one day to live up to our end of the bargain, and excuse me, but I wasn't informed about any plans to secure their whereabouts," I said.

"It wasn't your place to know." Alon assessed me. "It was being worked out," he said with an exhale. "We had a more pressing timeline that needed our attention, which is now ruined because of your little escapade. An excellent warrior is dead and two others, plus the princess's father, are in the hands of Madden." His shoulders pulled back.

I lowered my head. "I'm aware."

"I thought I trained you better than this."

My gaze stayed on the floor. It felt like a knife pierced my heart. "I will do better."

"You will have the chance to prove it to me." My head snapped up, and Alon moved around to the back of his desk. "We need to send the princess to the kingdom of Nefali."

"Why, sir?" I asked, furrowing my brow.

"They have requested her presence in exchange for their support in the war against Madden." Alon waved a letter in the air. "She was meant to arrive today."

Pressing my tongue to the roof of my mouth, I couldn't help the frustration I felt. "She would never have gone, not without her parents."

He pointed the letter in my direction. "That was never your concern."

Knock. Knock.

The door slowly opened to a disheveled Princess Talia. She hadn't changed her clothes, and her hair was in messy clumps upon her shoulders. Dark circles marred her eyes, but determination shone within them as she entered.

"I'm in," she said to Alon.

"Excuse me, Your Highness?" he asked, stepping out from his desk.

"I said, I'm in." She stopped next to me. There was something else different about her. "I'll be your lost princess, your beacon of hope for the upcoming war against King Madden." My face twisted as I tried to understand what was going on in her head. "On one condition."

"And what might that be?" Alon asked.

"We do things my way."

"Your High—"

"No," she lifted her palm up, "I'm done being someone's puppet. From now on I will have a say in every decision that is made. If you want me to become Landore's beacon of hope, then start by giving me some respect and authority."

My lips parted, unsure of how Alon would respond. He stood there for a moment, then placed his hands behind his back.

"Your Highness," he said with a bow.

"Good." Talia lifted her chin, but her eyes showed a hint of surprise. "First, I demand my father, Jules, and Gil be rescued immediately," she said like someone who had the authority to make such a demand, which I guess now she did.

"Of course," Alon said.

"Do I have your word that it will be your first priority?" she asked, emphasizing each word.

"Yes, Your Highness. Plans have already been discussed for their retrieval," he said with a small lift at the corner of his mouth.

I shook my head and looked at Talia. "Where is this coming from?" I asked, feeling like the only one completely confused by the sudden change in her.

Her eyes hardened as she turned to me. "He won't stop. He will never stop coming after the ones I love. The only way to guarantee my safety and those I care about is to eliminate him as a threat." Her hands tightened into fists. "It's time I did something to stop him."

"How correct you are, Your Highness. And he will be stopped," Alon said, pulling Talia's attention.

"Now, tell me of this plan to retrieve my father, Jules, and Gil," she said, pulling back her shoulders.

Alon smiled. "Yes, Your Highness."

Keep reading for a sneak peak at *The Rising*, book 4 in *The Calling* series.

THE RISING

BOOK FOUR IN
THE CALLING SERIES

L.C. PYE

CHAPTER 1

Talia

"No," I said, slamming my palm against the wooden table. "Until we have rescued all three of them, I refuse to go anywhere." Heat radiated off my skin. We had accomplished nothing in the past two hours. All they cared about was shipping me off to Nefali. We were no closer to a plan for rescue than when we arrived back in Aydencia two days ago.

"Your Highness, if I may?" Hanna spoke for the first time since the meeting had started. Her back pressed against the chair and her hands were folded in her lap. Dark circles outlined the bottom of her puffy eyes. It seemed I wasn't the only one who couldn't sleep. She bowed her head, waiting for my approval.

"Go ahead," I said. The knot in my stomach tightened even more. I wasn't comfortable with them treating me like a true royal. However, everyone had accepted my terms of allowing me to have a say in the decisions being made. A little too easily. I couldn't stop thinking that it had been their plan for me all along. That I would finally take the role of Princess Talia, heir to the throne of Landore, seriously. It was fine by me if they thought I had had a change of heart about becoming their future queen. I would let them know that I didn't have any intentions of becoming queen—after I got what I wanted.

Hanna looked at Richard with saddened eyes and then she turned her attention to me. "Richard and I are desperate to rescue them too, but we need to be smart about this. We can't endanger them more by rushing into this."

"I can't imagine how you and Richard feel." I held my breath. "But we aren't rushing into this. We know exactly what King Madden wants—me." The last word bounced off the stone walls, leaving a haunting echo.

Something rustled behind me. I didn't turn around. I knew who it was. I had been all too aware of his every breath for the past two hours. His movement most likely meant he disapproved of my plan to use myself as bait to rescue the others, but it wasn't his place to say anything. Raph's job was to stand behind me and be my bodyguard. A role I tried to lobby for *anyone* else to have, but Alon refused to compromise on this point when accepting my terms.

"Your Highness, that's not an option," Alon said from between me and Richard. We were in Skyhall in a room deep within the mountain. They seemed to only use it as a place for meetings because nothing other than a large fireplace and the circular table and chairs occupied the space.

"Of course it is," I said.

"It's not an option we will entertain." His eyes hardened and then softened a fraction. "We will not risk your life."

"But you're willing to risk Gil's, Jules's, and my father's lives?"

Richard grasped Hanna's hand. "We must think of the endgame," Richard said. His gaze fixed on me, but it was as if he was saying the words to his wife. Hanna pulled her hand away and placed it back in her lap. "Before we can storm the palace, we need to ensure we will defeat Madden. We need to be sure we have the manpower to take on his guards, and the power to silence anyone who might think the throne is up for the taking, which is why we need aid from the Kingdom of Nefali." Richard extended his hand toward Hafsa and Nadav, the last two sitting at the table. "With the Kingdom of Nefali backing you, no one would dare try to fight your claim to the throne."

"I understand our need for their support, and I'm willing to do my part, but why must we wait to rescue the others?" I grabbed the fabric of my pants and readied myself to share my plan with them. "Instead, we can offer King Madden a treaty with the Northern Rebels. We'll use it as a cover. Then, while I'm discussing the terms with him," a sharp inhale came from behind me along with multiple sets of eyes widening, "a team can go in and retrieve them." I ignored Raph and looked at Alon expectantly. I had worked through the plan all night, but I hoped they would've had their own solution so I wouldn't even have to offer mine as an option. It was risky, but it could work.

Alon steepled his fingers against his lips. "And why do you think Madden will go along with this peace treaty, Your Highness?" he asked.

"Because we are going to give him what he wants—control."

"Continue." He lowered his hands, finally seeming interested.

"We will promise to disperse the Northern Rebels."

A loud laugh broke out. "You can't be serious?" Richard asked with raised eyebrows. "Your Highness," he bowed his head, "he will never take your word on that. He will want evidence that the Northern Rebels are no more. He will want blood."

"Not if he believes the rebels support him as king," I said.

"And how would you achieve that?"

"By marrying Prince Kasper."

Noises broke out in the room, but the sound of Raph clearing his throat rang the loudest.

"Absolutely not," Richard said, throwing up his arms.

"You can't," Hafsa said as she shared a concerned look with Nadav.

"Everyone, relax. I won't go through with any of it. Like I said, it will be a cover."

"Let me get this straight. You plan to use a peace treaty as a cover to deceive King Madden. You'd use the same tactic he used when he killed the royal fam—your family?"

"Yes," I answered, trying to hide the smile that dared escape. The poetic justice of it was my favorite part of the plan.

"Alon, you can't be considering this," Richard said.

Alon ignored Richard and kept his focus on me. "Your Highness, your plan carries merit, but there are too many risks that we can't afford to take." I opened my mouth, but Alon lifted his hand to silence me. "Not solely because you're the center of this plan, but we also don't know if Madden is holding them at the palace."

I closed my mouth. I hadn't thought of that.

"What I suggest is that we send our best team of warriors to do some reconnaissance and confirm that they're being held in the palace. After their location is confirmed, we can go forward with a rescue plan."

"Yes, but that will take too much time." I pressed my lips into a thin line. Who knew what torture they were enduring already at the hands of King Madden and Prince Kasper?

"We can lose time. We cannot lose you," Alon said. I got ready to argue but then bit my tongue as I looked around the room. They would never agree to putting the "lost princess" in danger.

"In the meantime, you can accompany Hafsa and Nadav to Nefali," Richaid chimed in. I wanted to roll my eyes. Of course, he wouldn't drop that. "If word comes back that Madden is holding them in the palace, then we can proceed with an extraction plan. By then you will have the support of a whole kingdom, so we can save not only your father, Gil, and Jules, but we can take out Madden at the same time."

I bit my tongue, not letting my true emotions show. "Okay." There was no point in arguing because we would just end up back at the beginning with no action plan.

"It's a plan," Richard said, and he relaxed visibly as if a weight had been lifted off his shoulders. A weight that seemed to have moved to my shoulders. I needed to come up with a plan on how to join the team headed to the palace.

"Raph, do you think your contacts in Llycia might help?" Alon asked.

I couldn't stop myself from turning this time. Jules had mentioned that they worked with street orphans to help rescue me, but Alon couldn't be referring to them. Raph's face tightened. Or maybe he was...

"Yes. I can touch base with them when I arrive in Llycia," Raph answered.

"No. You will escort Princess Talia with Nadav and Hafsa to Nefali," Alon said.

Raph's eyes flicked to me. My stomach tightened. The emotion that crossed his face was too hard to decipher before he focused on Alon. We hadn't talked directly to each other since we returned to Aydencia. I'd been doing all I could to make sure we were never alone. Heat flared to my cheeks at the thought of his obvious regret at kissing me.

"We will send Adira and a team to Llycia. Will they be willing to work with Adira?" Alon looked at Raph.

"Yes. She gained their trust during our time there."

"It's settled. We will have a team sent as soon as possible. Nadav?" Alon dipped his head in Nadav's direction.

"Word was sent yesterday of our request for a convoy." Nadav glanced hesitantly in my direction. There was something in his expression that was unnerving, as if he was worried.

"Wonderful. You can leave for Nefali the moment we hear word that a convoy has been sent to meet you halfway," Richard said, in high spirits. However, he seemed to be the only one fully on board with the new plan. There was a heaviness in the room that seemed to be affecting everyone else.

"Your Highness," Alon broke the silence, "I suggest you inform your mother."

I hadn't even thought about how this would separate us again. There was no way they would allow her to come, and honestly, I didn't want her to. Where I was planning to go was somewhere she wouldn't be safe.

"You are dismissed." Alon placed his hands on the table and stood. "Richard, please send Adira to my study."

Everyone stood and exited the room. I quickened my steps toward the women's hall, needing to pretend that I was going back to my room before I headed back to Alon's study. If I planned to sneak onto the ship with Adira and the team headed to Llycia, I needed to know the details.

As I entered the main entryway, the sound of boots hitting the stone floor echoed around me. My thoughts had distracted me, and I forgot about my newly appointed shadow. I glanced back to see Raph closing the distance between us.

"You don't have to follow me. We're in Skyhall, and I'm going to my room. Nothing will happen," I said over my shoulder.

"Your Highness, as your guard, I must ensure your safety in all places. Even when we assume we are among friends."

I turned and halted. "Does someone here want to hurt me?" I asked, crossing my arms.

Raph stopped inches from me, then he took a step back. "Not that I'm aware of, Your Highness. I'm just being cautious," he finished with a bow of his head.

I dropped my arms and clenched my hands into fists, wanting to punch him in the face. It was as if he saw me strictly as an assignment from Alon and nothing else. Like being near me wasn't hard for him in the slightest. Meanwhile, the knife in my heart dug deeper every time I saw him. His demeanor confirmed that he regretted the kiss even though he had kissed me first.

"I agreed to let you be my guard so that if I'm attacked, you can protect me." I wasn't naïve. I still had a lot to learn when it came to self-defense. "But that is all I agreed to. I don't need you breathing down my neck every second and making not-so-subtle hints that you don't agree with me. That is not your role." I held his gaze, wanting him to fully understand me. "I need space."

His eyes softened.

My anger flared. He didn't get to feel sorry for me. I didn't want his sympathy. I wanted to get over him—even if it felt like that would never happen. Every time I closed my eyes, I felt his lips against mine and the way he held onto me as if I was the air he needed to breathe. The kiss had been rough and full of need. And it would haunt me forever.

"Princess, we should talk."

That was not going to happen. I couldn't survive another rejection from him.

I looked past him.

He whipped his head around, and I took off down the women's hall. It was childish, and he would be right behind me again in seconds, but I didn't care. I needed space, which was another reason my plan to go to Llycia was genius. There would be no Raph.

I opened my door and slammed it shut before Raph could catch up. My breathing was erratic as I leaned against the door. It was as if all the running Adira and Hafsa made me do in our training sessions had been pointless. I dropped my head back with a thud. How long would I have to wait before I could leave? I wouldn't put it past Raph to station himself outside my door.

Knock. Knock.

I jumped away from the door and clutched my chest. My frustration quickly turned to anger. He needed to take the hint. I wanted to be alone. Wind brushed against my face as I threw the door open, ready to command Raph to leave me alone.

"Oh. Mother," I said, blinking rapidly. "I thought you were someone else."

"I see that," she said. "I heard your door slam and wanted to be sure you were okay. May I come in?"

"This isn't the best time. I was—"

"Talia, there is something I need to tell you." Her eyes dropped to the floor as she wrung her hands together. I had never seen her like this. My heart rate picked up again.

"What is it?" I stepped out of the way to allow her in. I closed the door slowly, trying to prepare myself for whatever she was about to say.

"Let's sit." She moved over to the bed and patted the space next to her.

"Mother, you're scaring me."

She didn't speak.

"What is it?" I asked.

"It's about the night you were found."

My anxiety lowered, but barely, as her body stayed tense. "What about that night?"

"We said you were abandoned in the forest until a group of Hunters found you..."

"Right, then you and Father offered to adopt me. I know the story." We didn't talk about that night often, but growing up, Jacob Martin never let me forget it. How my own parents hadn't even wanted me.

"Well. The thing is..." She licked her lips and swallowed. "That's not exactly what happened."

I lowered my chin. "What *exactly* happened then?"

"I found you in the forest that day."

"Why would you lie about that?"

"When I found you," her expression twisted as if she was fighting with herself on the inside, "you weren't alone."

DELETED CHAPTER OF KASPER'S POV

Want to know what happened after Prince Kasper woke up from the sleeping tonic?
Download here:

ACKNOWLEDGMENTS

This year hasn't been easy, but I've received so much love and encouragement from my readers that I can confidently say *The Choosing* would never have been published without them. The random messages telling me how much you enjoyed *The Calling* series has fueled me to keep going.

All honor and credit goes to my Heavenly Father. He gives me the heart and inspiration to keep writing, and I want to give all glory to Him.

To my husband, Matt, who has supported me through every up and down and continues to help me pursue this dream by being my biggest supporter. Love you so much, babe, always and forever.

To my family: you have always been and will continue to be my biggest supporters (even though you really have no choice). I am extremely grateful for each of you.

To my street team: I don't know how to show you my gratitude. Your support and love for not only my books, but for me as a person, is mind-blowing. You have been so understanding with my slower pace this year and have encouraged me every step of the way. Your excitement for this series is infectious. Thank you for believing in me.

To my readers: I hope you have enjoyed *The Choosing*! If you have, please SHARE the love with others. The best way to support me is to spread the word to your friends or with a review/rating on Amazon or Goodreads. Also, please reach out. I would love to know your thoughts and get to know you!

To my beta reader/developmental editor: Jade Lawson, I can't thank you enough. You're a true blessing, and I'm forever grateful for how you have helped me develop this series to where it's at now. Thank you for your honest feedback and advice, and more so, your continual support of the series.

To my editor: Brittany Ortega at E&A Editing Services, you are more than I could have ever asked for. This is the third time I have worked with you, and I'm so glad you were able to fit me into your schedule. You went beyond my expectations and were there for me every step of the way. You tightened up my writing and made sure this book fit in with the rest of the series. Thank you for your constant support and belief in my writing!

About Author
L.C. Pye

L.C. Pye is a South Carolina-based author of YA novels. She grew up in North Dakota, then moved to Australia for four years after college. She met her husband there, and in 2018, they moved to the Carolinas. She has spent most of her life creating stories through the art of dance. But after a dream in 2019, she decided to try telling her stories through words.

L.C. has had the privilege of traveling to many different countries, and she loves to put those differing but beautiful cultures into her writing. She hopes all of her readers will experience the same beauty she has through her books.

Connect with L.C.
Website: www.lcpye.com
Instagram: @l.c.pye
TikTok: @l.c.pye
Email: authorl.c.pye@gmail.com